THE DARK COMPANION

With good wishes
from the author
18 Sept 2010

THE DARK COMPANION

Ghost Stories

JOHN GASKIN

THE LILLIPUT PRESS
DUBLIN

First published 2001 by
THE LILLIPUT PRESS LTD
62–63 Sitric Road, Arbour Hill,
Dublin 7, Ireland
www.lilliputpress.ie

A CIP record for this title is available from
The British Library.

1 3 5 7 9 10 8 6 4 2

ISBN 1 901866 79 3

Set in Hoefler Text with Verdana display titles
Printed by Betaprint, Clonshaugh, Dublin

CONTENTS

PREFACE & ACKNOWLEDGMENTS

The earliest of these stories took its beginning from an account written in my diary in 1959; the latest was finished in 1999. They were in fact all designed originally to be read aloud: some at small gatherings in schools or colleges, some in private houses at New Year, some on the BBC, and one as a caution to myself.

With one exception (historical figures apart), none of the characters bear any resemblance to persons living or dead. The exception is a wise and distinguished scholar who did indeed meet a strange death shortly after my story was written. But if the characters and some of the events are fictitious, the places are not, and they may all be found by those who have eyes to see.

Why do I, a sceptical academic philosopher, write ghost stories? I suppose it is because I enjoy – in a certain way – the cloistered and cosy chill which is to be found in following out the consequences of possible evil, the consistent ambiguities in things, the worlds we can unlock with our own feelings, or the unnoticed coincidences: between death and beautiful teeth perhaps. I trust others may find enjoyment – of a certain sort – in reading them.

It is unlikely that I would have had the temerity to continue writing such stories as these without the encouragement of Paul Durcan in 1990, and J.V. Luce at numerous times in our long association. It is a certainty that, without the skill and patience of Ciara de Mora in transcribing my manuscripts when she could have been doing more interesting things, this book would not be in existence. To them, and particularly to her, are due my abiding thanks.

JOHN GASKIN
Trinity College Dublin & Northumberland

THE DARK COMPANION

The Pit

You will be a wise man if you stop up your ears. The
song which Ulysses feared was alluring, but came not
from every side; the song which you have to fear
echoes round you not from a single headland but
from every quarter of the world.

Seneca, *On Sirens' Voices*

Two figures crossed the fields. Behind them the house. Ahead
the valley to left and right. Their shadows stretched out
towards it, dark and long in the evening sunshine. One was that of
a small, middle-aged man in tweeds made for the country rather
than of the country. The other belonged to a tall casually dressed
girl who would soon be strikingly beautiful (as most of the girls
and some of the boys at her fashionably co-educational boarding
school had already noticed).

"It's hard to imagine *that* with iron rails and trucks and so on,"
she said, pointing to a scarcely visible line on the pasture slopes
below.

3

The man beside her made an effort to look, but his attention moved on, across the tops of trees and the shrunken stream below them, up the banks of crumbling shale and scrub barred with lines of sandstone on the far side of the valley, and away into the empty moorland beyond. Uncomfortable, worthless land, he thought.

"It was closed about 1927," she chattered on, "after the mine flooded. Or so I'm told. If you look out to the right – " Here she took the man's arm. It did not require an effort to be captivated by her touch. "If you look out to the right you'll see where the wagonway – I think that's what pit railways were called – where it got to the top of the valley. It joined the ordinary railway about two miles farther on. There are no trains now. Dad remembers them. There was a pit manager's house too, and miners' cottages. But they've gone like everything else around here."

She turned the other way. For a moment the man was free to observe the late August sun catching the dark lights of black and red in her hair and the lines of her body, then she was directing his attention again.

"Now look down there. Yes, in the trees, by the Routing Burn. Two pits were in there, just above flood level, or so they thought. Would you like to have a look? Dad would never let me and Elizabeth go there but ... there's time before dinner. We might find mushrooms," she ended hurriedly.

"Thank you Julia." The nicely bred vowels of Edinburgh Morningside were much in evidence. "If it is safe, a quick look might be interesting. We needn't tell your father," he added.

Robert Caleb, bachelor by default and financial consultant in an important provincial city by choice, was in most respects a successful man and knew it. One of his failings was that he couldn't resist making money for himself, and for other people if they paid him enough. It was therefore unsurprising that a chance encounter with a certain Major Sutherton at a business lunch should have led to an invitation for a weekend's golf – unsurprising given the fact that Julia Sutherton's father was intent upon a property development in a town whose Planning Officer was heavily obliged to Robert Caleb and Partners. "Just a weekend in the country, a bit of golf and a walk," Caleb had said to his secretary as he left the office on the Friday evening. When, therefore, at the conclusion of their business, Major Sutherton had suggested that his daughter might show Robert a little of the country before dinner, he could scarcely refuse – especially in view of one of his other failings.

With Julia leading, they reached the old track, now no more than a ledge on the grass slopes. Turning left, they followed its shallow gradient down, Caleb walking a little closer to the girl than was perhaps necessary, until they were forced apart by the need to duck under hazel bushes and tread down nettles and brambles where the track disappeared under the trees at the narrow foot of the valley.

"It isn't far," Julia assured him gaily as she held aside the runners of a wild rose which trailed like razor-wire across the way. "But mind your leg on this stuff."

On one side, the bank pressed against them with slopes of collapsing earth, looped and stitched with the roots of trees that groped out of the ground like arthritic bones. On the other side, the remains of the track crumbled into the burn. Caleb could hear the water gurgling and sucking under great blocks of stone which were still draped over with the grey debris left by winter floods. At intervals the stream appeared in deep pools overhung with lush ferns and trailing branches, its far side a cascade of stones and mud in which sickly birch and ash had taken precarious root. If he had not felt the animal excitement of the girl urging him on, he would have turned back. It would have been wiser. He had little taste for the country, but enough to sense that he was in an ugly, smothered place, from which man had retreated after his violence, and to which the wild had greedily returned.

The end of the way came abruptly. The river turned left under the track and then, after briefly widening out into a shallow, disappeared into a gorge overhung with trees. At their feet roughly cut stones marked the abutments of what had been a bridge. On the far side – about twenty feet away – the line terminated in a deep clearing confined by damp cliffs into which beech trees had somehow dug their roots so that the trunks grew up hard against the rock. In the middle, and directly ahead, a broken fence enclosed a small patch of blackthorn and elder out of which the dead arms of an ash sapling reached up to the circle of sky that fitted over the place like a lid.

"That's it," said the girl. "The shaft's in that lot of bushes. It's easy to get across down there." She pointed to the shallows below the missing bridge. "Go and have a look."

"I think, Julia," Caleb began, "that it's a little late and your father –"

"Oh do have a look Mr Caleb! You aren't frightened are you? It's perfectly safe if you don't –"

"Of course not. I wouldn't go near it if I thought it wasn't safe. I was simply thinking of your mother's cooking. But I see it is only six o'clock." Then he added after a slight pause, "Are you coming with me?"

"I've not got wellies on," she remarked glancing at her dusty white trainers. "You have. We'll go together next time."

Left to himself, Caleb would have acted differently. But he was not left to himself. He was the object of attention by a fifteen-year-old girl. It would, he reasoned with himself, be interesting, just a little intriguing. He had never seen a long-abandoned pit shaft. It

6

would probably be filled in ... and the crossing was easy – and the next time when they went together he would know the way.

It was quiet, very quiet, on the far side, as if the stream had been swallowed up behind him. The turf was short and sear. Possibly it grew on thinly covered rock or old slag flattened out round the pit head. Julia was standing where he had left her, watching him, her face half-hidden in long skeins of dark red hair.

"Go on," she called across to him.

The bushes round the pit head were motionless. Only the tops of the great trees above the clearing moved slightly. He leaned forward, holding the branches on both sides. There was a dark area beyond the dead ash. He pushed another cautious step into the undergrowth. It was there: an unguarded nondescript hole, seven or eight feet square – rather smaller than he had anticipated. Over the edge festoons of withered grass dangled like strings. Fragments of timber, relics of old cladding perhaps, sagged away from the sides. He peered hesitatingly into the darkness. A stench of raw earth and rotting wood drifted up. He thought he saw the bottom, maybe forty, maybe sixty feet below. It was hard to say. And there was a vague area of ... possibly mud ... and sticks ... yes, sticks or the bones of a dead sheep ... and an object like a coconut only larger ... almost certainly a stone.

He drew back with a sudden uneasiness. The place was dangerous, and it gave him the curious impression that nothing had moved or been moved for a very long time; as if the winter floods had never reached the clearing again, nor the winds disturbed the dead grass. Such fanciful feeling was entirely strange to Caleb, and as he returned to where Julia was standing he was just a little suspicious that his nice existence had been deliberately disturbed by a mischievous errand. But exactly in what way it had been mischievous eluded him.

"Well?" she said.

"Nothing to see. Only a hole with rubbish in it as you would expect. But dangerous. I hope you never go there?"

"No one does. It's forbidden."

"Why hasn't it been filled in?"

She shrugged. "It's fenced off from sheep at the top of those cliffs and only locals know it's here. I don't expect anyone's looked down it for years."

There was a note in her voice which made Caleb wish he could see her expression. But that was not possible beneath the dark vaulting of the trees. Without saying anything more she turned and led the way back up the track. He began to follow her, but she was moving too fast for him. Behind them, at the shaft head, the branches he had disturbed edged almost imperceptibly back into position again and then moved uneasily, as if by the agency of one of those inexplicable adjustments of air that can somehow emerge from nothing on a summer evening, and as quickly disperse into stillness. An observer might have been forgiven for thinking that an animal of some kind was about to emerge, but Caleb did not look back to see. He was concentrating upon the girl. She was scrambling up the track as if to escape him rather than lead him home. He tried to speed up but she moved faster than ever. She was trying to leave him behind. At the edge of the trees she stopped. Hot and bordering on anger, he caught up with her.

"There's no hurry!" he gasped.

"I thought we might be late for dinner. Mummy is so fussy," she said airily.

Caleb glanced at his watch. There was still plenty of time. She had deliberately contrived to make him chase her, or so it felt. Or she had run away from him, or from the place, or something. Whatever it was, Caleb felt in need of an explanation.

8

"What was it like?" she asked before he could speak. "I felt a bit frightened when you disappeared. Is it full of water?" – again the curious edge to her voice.

"No I don't think so. Just rubbish of some sort. Branches and things. I couldn't really see." He was trying to formulate a question about her sudden departure, but her next remark checked him again.

"Don't tell Daddy I took you there. He doesn't realize I'm not a child any longer and he'd fuss."

"Of course not. It can be our little secret." He spoke without thinking, and added quickly, "But you'll not go back there alone?"

"I won't, don't worry!" The sense of cosy conspiracy hung for a moment between them, then she added, "Shall we go for a walk in the early morning? It's super up on the heather at dawn. Dad's always too lazy and I have to get up early to exercise Pinto."

"Er ... yes, if you like. If it's fine. I generally take a little walk before breakfast." He stumbled on, excusing himself too eagerly into the commitment. "I have to play a game of golf with your father at about eleven while your mother is at church. But earlier on, yes, certainly. If you can waken in time."

She glanced at him contemptuously. "Of course I can waken," she said. "I expect I'll have to come for you."

They spoke little while climbing out of the valley. The girl seemed to have withdrawn into her own world, and Caleb's thoughts moved away into a tax-saving calculation which was surprisingly soothing. They had crossed two of the three fields on the return to the house when he looked back. The setting sun caught the underside of the trees and hedges so that vivid outlines in gold and green shone against a dark background like one of the lush pictures in a *Country Life* calendar.

"It's only a cow," said Julia.

9

"What is?"

"Oh sorry. I thought you were looking at that thing down there. I thought it was somebody following us, but I've been deceived like that before in this sort of light. A sheep coughing can sound just like a man as well you know."

"Can it?" Caleb turned away. It was unimportant. He was looking forward to the lights of the house. The sun was low on the hills beyond it. The garden opened towards them. He was thinking about dinner. And then he was thinking again about his host's daughter, and not at all about anything she might have seen.

*

Woodlee, the major's house, stood on its own grounds about three miles from the nearest village, the single spacious lawn at the rear opening east towards the valley of the Routing Burn between high hedges and borders of dahlias, lupins and delphiniums. The house itself, built in 1920 for a munitions baron, and probably designed originally for Middlesex rather than the north, was spread across the width of the garden: an affluence of gables, leaded lights, verandas and French windows picked out from the cream-washed walls in a black similitude of Tudor oak. At the front a yellow gravel drive led away from the assortment of double garages and cedar looseboxes on one side of the main entrance, through a wind-blown apology for a shrubbery, and out onto the public road. Beyond the road, heather and stone dykes and the laughter of grouse met the inhabitants of Woodlee.

The dining-room opened onto the garden. After dinner it was so warm that Caleb, together with Major Sutherton (RA, retired), Sutherton's wife and Elizabeth, their youngest daughter, now thirteen and at the transitional stage between spots, horses and boyfriends, sat on the veranda – the adults smoking and drinking coffee. Julia had gone to her room saying she wanted to listen to a CD, but the company was augmented by Dr Ellis, the local GP, and his wife, and a couple of week-enders from the village, the male half of whom was "in publishing", while his consort prospered as a species of social psychologist.

"Don't you feel lonely out here?" she had just asked Elizabeth.

"It's all right. There's plenty to do in the summer and we're back to awful school before you can say moo."

"It's the security angle that would worry me," put in the publisher half. "Nowhere seems to be safe these days."

"We keep two dogs," murmured Mrs Sutherton, a sensitive woman made nervous by her husband.

"Damned nuisance they are too. Have to exercise the brutes every morning," he barked.

"O Daddy, you know you *love* them," exclaimed Elizabeth. "Anyway nothing ever happens here." There was evident regret in her voice.

"Would you like some coffee Robert?" enquired Mrs Sutherton.

The question found Caleb dreaming. The trouble was that his chair was so placed that he could look straight down the lawn and into the fields to the east. The evergreens were black with the approach of night that always seemed to come to them first, but an afterglow in the west, coming from the other side of the house, still made it possible to distinguish tree and hedge. Someone was standing at the gate they had used on their return. It could not be Julia since he could hear the brutal jiggle of a rap lyric somewhere above their heads. He peered out past the conversation into the dusk. It might be a small horse facing them, a black and white horse, piebald, Pinto perhaps.

"Robert, would you like some more coffee? Robert!"

"I'm sorry. Forgive me. I wasn't attending. Nothing more, thank you."

"I think you were spying on a courting couple down the garden, Bob" the publisher suggested, laughing.

"Not at all Mr er ... I had a heavy day yesterday and I regret to say I was day-dreaming. I apologize."

"I can assure you", said the major, "that nobody could be out there. I haven't shut the dogs up yet and they'd be baying like hounds on a good line if we had visitors. Anyway, we've got no neighbours – not since the miners packed their bags years ago. Circulate the port will you."

"You know about those mines?" asked Dr Ellis.

"Do tell us," pleaded the psychologist. "I'm *so* interested in working-class sub-culture."

"I don't know anything about their culture, sub or otherwise. I presume they were ordinary men with thoughts and feelings like the rest of us, but the whole show folded up in a double drama: a flood and a –"

"Elizabeth, could you perhaps go upstairs and ask Julia to turn her gramophone down?" It was Mrs Sutherton who interrupted. "I can scarcely hear Dr Ellis speaking. "I'm sorry Dr Ellis, do go on. Yes, please go *now*, Elizabeth."

"Well, I was just saying the mines were flooded in a sudden thaw, in 1927 I think it was, and they never got the workings open again. Since there was no work for the men anywhere else they lingered up at Ember Terrace until the war, and the manager lingered on at his house up the valley from here. That was what led to the second drama. He lived alone, and nasty stories began to circulate about his tastes – one of them being the daughter of one of the ex-miners. The trouble was she was only thirteen. Well, maybe that sort of thing happens now – indeed I know it does – but it didn't then, and the girl's father gathered some of his mates together one night 'to sort him out' as they put it, and bring the girl home. She was living with him you see, but whether for love, or money, or out of fear of her father no one seemed sure. Anyway, when they got there he was in the kitchen with an axe buried in the front of his skull. He should have been dead, but made a recovery of a sort and lived – if that is the right word – for several more years in an institution."

"What about the girl?" asked the publisher.

"She had gone. She probably thought she had killed him, and to all intents and purposes she had. They thought she might have fled to one of the big cities although there was no report of her on the roads or on the train the night the body was discovered. The Blitz came shortly afterwards. If she'd reached London or Coventry or any of several possible places, she could easily have been killed unknown to anyone. On the other hand she could still be alive somewhere. We'll probably never know."

"What sort of girl was she?" enquired the psychologist.

"I've really no idea. It was all before my time. I've heard my father say she was like a big Irish tinker – all red hair and white skin that burnt in the sun – but if she was, she would have had dreadful difficulty hiding herself."

"But couldn't someone else have killed him?" persisted the psychologist. "The father, for example. Why automatically blame the girl?"

"Because all the men involved had been together for some time before, and what seemed to be the girl's fingerprints were on the axe."

"Couldn't the father have killed the girl earlier in a fit of anger and then attacked the manager? He could easily have hidden the body in a country he knew. Family anger can produce strange results."

"I dare say, and I'm sure you would know. Many hypotheses can fit the same facts. It's a matter of what is the simplest, most obvious."

As the doctor finished speaking Elizabeth returned to the room and although Mrs Sutherton didn't quite make a request, the conversation obligingly turned to other things to which once again Caleb found it difficult to attend. He was tired both as a result of the day and from a recent bout of flu that had left him with a tendency to exhaustion in the later evening. After another half hour or so he contrived to excuse himself out of the company. He had apologized to his hostess in advance, and she had been most understanding. Elizabeth had gone to bed already.

On his way upstairs he paused at the open window of the landing. The night had cooled but there was no sign of the rain that the land desperately needed. He looked down into the garden again. Something vaguely unpleasant was still at the gate. He hesitated, then with a quick movement shut the window and pulled the curtain cord. Julia's room was just along the corridor. He must pass it on the way to his own. She was still listening to CDs. "I wanna ... wanna ... wanna ..." The rest was lost in drumming and rhythmic grunts. He closed his own door. He knew what he wanted, and would contrive if he could. He wanted –. Abruptly the disk ended and he was alone in the silence.

Most of the bedrooms, his own included, opened onto the back of the house with a prospect of garden, fields, valley and then remoter moorland beyond. But as Caleb closed the window against the moths and thunder flies and other unwanted items of country life, he could see none of these things. There was only his own reflection in the black glass and the lighted room behind him. He pulled the curtains. The country was vastly overrated. It suffered from lack of privacy. Everything was conspicuous. Even one's thoughts seemed to be observable.

He undressed slowly, unable to rid himself of a confusion of fears and temptations, and of the sense that he ought not to have been dared – for that was what it amounted to – into poking about the old mine shaft. Damn the girl! Why had she wanted him to look into it? To tell her what he had seen. His thoughts closed all too easily over what he had seen. He could see it again now. Dead sticks and an old turnip which turned into a face like a Halloween mask as he looked at it. With an effort he pulled his mind away. He had an important meeting on the Monday morning with old George McKerrow, and its subject matter was profitable enough to divert his attention even from the fear of Woodlee.

He lay down as the party below began to break up. A car started at the front of the house, and then there were the sounds of the Suthertons going to bed. He lay still, and thought, and turned over, and fidgeted. Even the solace of George McKerrow's news failed him, and a large moth was bumping and patting at the window. He debated whether to get up and kill it, but the things were everywhere and others would return. Rest there seemed to be none, but at intervals he must in fact have slept, for he dreamed luridly – the suffocating, sick dreams that Camembert, and port, and an overfull stomach can inflict on a middle-aged man. And in this maelstrom of images there was always a return to one: like shaking a kaleidoscope which had been programmed to reform itself around a single picture that reached out to him, luring him into some dreadful darkness. Then he began to be conscious of the windows again as faint oblongs on one side of the room. He was being called. The sound, he was sure, had come from outside.

Normally he would have been very unwilling to get up at that hour, but almost anything would be an improvement on a continuation of those dreams. He looked out. A grey bar of cloud lay over the eastern hills and a monochrome twilight formed the still prelude to a summer dawn. Julia was standing at the far side of the field beyond the garden beckoning to him. What possessed the girl to get up so early was beyond his comprehension, but she clearly wanted him to come. The beckoning was unmistakable. He raised a hand in acknowledgment. She had said she would call him, but he hadn't appreciated she had intended it to be *that* early. He couldn't not go, but he hoped nobody would notice. It was just a bit *too* early for decency.

He hurried into his clothes. When he looked out of the window again she was still there – two fields away, standing thin and forlorn by the gate where he thought he had seen the horse the previous evening. He crept downstairs and let himself quietly out of the French windows, hoping as he did so that the dogs would not raise an unseemly commotion. Clearly she had not disturbed them, but then they knew her.

*

Julia spent a blissfully easy night. After washing her hair and listening to one of the When's latest hits, she had rolled up in her duvet and almost instantly gone to sleep. Her eyes opened to read 5:40 on the digital face of her radio alarm.

She was not sure why she had wakened. Something unusual had intruded on her sleep. She listened. Possibly one of the dogs had barked. Or a door had shut. She rolled aside the duvet and sprang to the window. It was full light but sunless. Then a movement in the field beyond the garden end caught her attention: old

Mr Caleb walking swiftly away from her. She knew his prim little trot. But he had waved to someone. She could see empty fields and nothing more. Perhaps he had misunderstood? He was to have gone for a walk with her. She would then again try to find out what he had seen at the pit. Since her forbidden experiment some weeks ago she had been feeling guilty and worried. She didn't know what she had seen there, but it had frightened her, and she wanted someone else to look and tell her it was all right. Rubbish, he had said; but that was not all.

Not really thinking what she should do, she pulled on jeans and a T-shirt and slipped down the stairs. On her way through the hall she grabbed one of her mother's hideous knitted hats – an evil assortment of browns and reds –and wound an old fawn scarf of her own about her neck. The morning could be cold. A further idea occurred to her. She would be walking straight into the rising sun if it appeared, and Elizabeth had just given her sunglasses for her birthday. She slipped them self-consciously on, and made to follow him. He couldn't have been meeting someone else? Possibly he ... anyway she could catch him. But as she went into the new-ness of the dawn she saw to her dismay that he was already well across the last of the fields which lay between the house and the pastures sloping down to the Routing Burn. She did not like to shout since that would raise a clamour from the dogs, and proba-bly fetch her father. Anyway, Mr Caleb was rather far away to hear. She set out at a steady jog. As she climbed the stile at the end of the garden a dog barked.

*

Although Major Sutherton had made light of intruders, he was a prudent man who took no real warning lightly. Gled had barked.

The voice of the big Labrador was unmistakable. Reluctantly he climbed out of bed, leaving his wife asleep, and looked out of the window without moving the curtains more than an inch or two. For a few moments nothing caught his attention. It was a still, grey, slightly damp morning, and no one was about. Then, to his chagrin, he saw his elder daughter walking quickly away from the house across a field. He was not so much surprised as annoyed. She was a wilful person, but he had told her to be careful about going anywhere alone at her age. There were queer folk even in the country. Evidently she was walking with a purpose. For a brief moment he contemplated the storm he would provoke if he followed her. Better a child's anger than a parent's regret he thought, and the dogs would give him an excuse. They were clearly restive. He pulled on his clothes as quickly as he could and tiptoed down to the boot cupboard. Even so, it took him some time to spot her when he went outside. She was just disappearing over the slopes. He released the dogs from their kennel, clipped them onto a leash in case they disturbed his sheep, and set out after Julia at a vigorous pace, far from pleased at a walk in the cobwebby damp of the early hours.

*

When Caleb had begun his pursuit, the questionable wisdom of what he was doing did not occur to him. She had asked him to go for a walk with her in the early morning, and there she was, beckoning him. Or had been when he set out, although he could no longer get a clear view across the fields, being down among them now, and his view obscured by hedgerows. He had at least escaped the dratted dogs. But his quarry had escaped him. He hurried on across the second field. Why was the wretched girl not waiting for him? She had said a walk in the heather – up at the other side of the house – not down here again in the shadows.

At the limit of the third field, when he could see down into the valley, he paused. Yes, she was there. A figure was waiting for him at the margin of the trees. He thought she was looking up at him. It was a trick of the queer light that made her look so odd. He could see her pale face beneath the red hair. Then again perhaps it was a hat. There was something about her head which was difficult to interpret. He drew breath to shout, and again thought better of it. In the silence his voice would carry for miles. It would not be discreet to shout. But she had called him. The voice was in his ears, strangely disembodied in the space of the valley, carrying with it all the sweetness and mockery of a child.

He reached the old wagonway, and turned to follow. A roe deer sprang from the path at his approach and fled across the land like the shadow of a cloud fleeing the sun. It did not interest him. Behind, far away, a dog barked. He did not turn. A fearful thought struck him. She was going to look at the shaft, and if she were to slip, or fall, or the edge to give way as it so easily could; or if some morbid, adolescent fantasy were to be lived out, what would he do? He was older. He would be responsible. Why had he been there? With what purpose had he followed her? Where precisely had he been at the time? He scrambled into the suffocating bushes and trees, the babble of hidden water muffling the sound of his progress.

He was calling now, but the sound would not carry properly through the foliage, and he could no longer see the way. A sort of panic was taking hold of him. He reached the missing bridge. There was no sign of her. A complete stillness hung over the clearing and, although he could see every detail of its emptiness in the quiet light, the impression remained that she was there, watching him. The panic subsided to be replaced by a shiver. He stared at the enclosure at the pit head. It was thicker at the centre than he remembered it. He mustn't alarm her by rushing. She was standing by the dead ash.

Moving carefully he made his way across the shallows as he had done the previous evening. There was no doubt at all that he faintly heard his name called, and the call was urgent, and the voice was unmistakably Julia's. He climbed up the bank, but could see nothing of her when he reached the clearing.

"Julia," he whispered, "are you there?"

No answer.

At the fence he paused, not knowing what to do. He couldn't leave her there, not *there*. If only his arms were long enough to take hold of her without going to the edge!

"Julia?"

Again silence. Something was very wrong. Fear pressed on him like a cold hand. He wanted to retreat, but like a man in a play he could not. He crossed the fence. The grass dangled undisturbed at the edges of the pit. Another step forward and he would see into it.

The light shone more clearly, but there was no one by the dead ash.

"Julia?" For the third time there came no whisper of reply to help him. Holding the ash for safety, he leaned forward.

The bottom of the shaft was empty. Far below, in the twilight of the earth, a few small stones lay on the mud. The sticks that were not sticks, and the dark patch that had not been a lump of wood, or a rock, or any of the other possibilities he had gone over in his mind, were not there. It was impossible. He held his breath. My god, what manner of thing had he followed? He was naked in the night, cold as death. A stick cracked behind him. A shadow joined his own at the mouth of the pit. In a sudden spasm of movement he turned far enough to see the brown head flecked with red, the darkened eye sockets and the place stopped with clay where there had been a mouth. Then he stepped back.

*

As Julia entered the trees she called on Mr Caleb. She was now absolutely at a loss to know what he was doing, and was becoming rather frightened. Why was he not waiting for her? Why not responding? As she advanced she heard his voice ahead, and to her dismay she realized he was calling her name. Something was very much wrong! How she knew it was wrong she didn't ask herself. Perhaps it was his voice. It didn't sound right. She hurried on, reaching the broken bridge in time to see him on the far side, standing with his back to her looking into the fenced bushes at the old shaft. She drew breath to call him and then didn't. An idea she didn't want had appeared in her mind, standing alongside her familiar thoughts, but not a product of them. She could surprise him. She could cross the water unobserved and come up behind him. He deserved it. She knew what he had wanted. She knew.

What happened then Julia never really understood, although she often thought about it and had to give some account of it to others. She *said* she tried to reach him. More accurately she found herself crossing the shallows, another purpose somehow superimposed upon, and controlling, her normal person. It was almost as though she were being impelled, as if her body had a movement independent of her real self. It took her onto the clearing and across the short turf to the fence, a few yards short of the pit.

He was still there. His back was towards her. He was intent upon something at the mouth of the pit. Her will could no longer restrain the stampeding hatred that was welling up inside her. She hated him and all men. They all knew. Her father knew. The anger burst out of her and towered over them both like the hammer of a god. She vaulted the fence. The shadow fell on him. He turned to face her. But he was not really facing her. Of that she was always certain. His eyes were not focused on her at all. They were fixed upon something to her left. His features were contorted, and he was crying from a mouth which hung open like the gash of a tragic mask. It was ugly, obscene. He was no more than a bare, sick, forked animal, and the earth was open behind him.

It was an advantage at the time that Major Sutherton was not in a position to know the details of what was happening. Knowledge might have disturbed him and delayed. As it was he could act freely on appearances. As he reached the end of the track he saw Julia standing in the clearing with her back to him looking at something in the bushes. Her very stance warned of danger. He had seen men stand thus when they were marking something for attack. Letting go of the dogs he crossed the burn at a run, shouting his daughter's name as he did so. Unusually, the two dogs did not follow him.

Julia never tried to tell her father what happened. There was an abrupt relaxation of tension in her head as if something had snapped, for a moment the thicket was a turmoil of cold air, then she was fighting for her life to drag Caleb back from the edge. For a dreadful moment he was taking her with him. He was already slipping. The edge was breaking away and he was fighting her. But he was small, and terror gave tremendous strength to her greater weight. Her heel caught in the grass and she fell back, away from the pit, dragging him down on top of her in the thorns and briars where he lay suddenly still.

The major found his daughter on her knees. She was sobbing

uncontrollably, her hat and sunglasses torn from her head, her bare legs lacerated by the fall. His useful business associate lay motionless on the ground by her side.

*

There is a little more to tell which may form a caution to the curious. Caleb was got back to Woodlee in a state of severe shock from which he emerged quite unable (or unwilling) to give any coherent account of what had happened. Julia was more forthcoming in matters of fact, but her father was left with a strong impression that not all she could have said had been said. Being an unimaginative man who dreaded emotional disturbance, he did not press the matter. The human bones which he had glimpsed at the bottom of the shaft were later identified as those of an unusually tall girl between twelve and sixteen years of age. Their attitude as photographed before removal, together with the pathologist's report, suggested (on the assumption that they had lain undisturbed since death) a fall resulting in a broken neck. The traces of rotting cloth discovered after a more thorough search, before the pit was filled in for safety, were uninformative. But the circumstantial evidence fitted so well with the disappearance of the girl before the war that local gossip was quite confident about a suicide or murder which the coroner merely pronounced probable. That the skeleton had only been observed after so long was attributed to the low water level resulting from exceptional drought, and to the fact that the place was very little visited.

It is perhaps fortunate, not from the point of view of the inquest, but from that of the reputation of Robert Caleb, that circumstances almost at once prevented him from having to bear witness that he had observed what must have been the bones on his first visit, but not when he looked, in better light, on his second. (It was especially fortunate since Major Sutherton would have had to testify with complete confidence that they were there, and recognizable as such when he looked moments later.) The circumstance which prevented Caleb was a drunken driver in charge of a large and powerful car: thus depriving the world at one blow of a very singular story and Robert Caleb & Partners of both its principal and its plurality – the other driver being one of his two partners.

The Black Knight

'Tis all a Chequer-board of Nights and Days
Where Destiny with Men for Pieces plays:
Hither and thither moves, and mates, and slays,
And one by one back in the Closet lays.

The Rubáiyát

What I have to tell is the record of an event inconsistent with all my experience both before and since, and as such I believe it may be of interest to others. The critical reader will complain that I should have spoken when my report could have been corroborated, at least in its attendant circumstances. But in those days I was young and unsure of myself, and as a junior fellow I had no wish to gain any reputation as a credulous dreamer.

I ought perhaps to begin by explaining that in the early 1960s a senior common room was a room or set of rooms provided in most universities for the exclusive use of the teachers or "dons" as they were then called. This was of course in the days when a real difference of academic attainment was still admitted to exist between teachers and students. As will be remembered by social historians, the distinction came to be regarded as divisive and was in reality destroyed by educational reforms at primary and secondary levels before it perished officially with the lately celebrated EU Tertiary Education (Equalization) Directive. However, at the time of which I speak, the distinction was still rigidly maintained. It extended even to social and cultural matters since it was assumed that those who performed well in the examination system still in vogue had thereby entitled themselves to comforts and luxuries not available to others.

In my own college – colleges were semi-autonomous, socio-residential teaching units grouped within the administrative ambit of certain ancient and pseudo-ancient universities – in my own college two rooms fulfilled the functions of a Senior Common Room; one large and Palladian, the other small by comparison, warm in the style of an old-fashioned study and accommodating to donnish comfort. On the October evening of which I am to speak (the precise date may be ascertained from an entry in the National Biographic Computer) there were few of us at dinner and we had withdrawn to the smaller room. It was a dark, cold night, and the room was pleasantly warmed by a large coal fire. It was lit by a group of candles on the sideboard and two standing electric lamps beside the fire. The most junior member present, Schwartz (who will be remembered for his work on the pigmentation of aphids), was pouring out coffee while I passed round the Madeira. Dr Ashton, our Senior Fellow and a man of great age and scholarship, was speaking to the Professor of Botany.

"Do you know, Lessop," he was saying, "how one should care for eucalyptus trees? I have several young ones in my garden and I haven't much experience of looking after them."

"You can't grow then outside in this country. Give them as

much shelter as you can. They might live a few months." The botanist was, I thought, gratuitously abrupt.

"A pity we didn't put eucalyptus instead of birch trees in the front of college when the elms died," murmured the older man as he sat down in his usual chair by the fire. He remained very still, looking into the flames.

The Senior Fellow had long since penetrated the confines of extreme old age. He had been at school under Queen Victoria and was an undergraduate in the early days of King Edward. For more than half a century he had been a Fellow of the College, watching the children's children come and go, watching the great institution of which he was a part grow and change until his youth would have scarcely recognized what his old age took for granted. His books filled a substantial shelf in most libraries, and in his day he had been soldier, sportsman, administrator and churchman as well as scholar. But his walk was still firm, his eye bright and his figure straight. Only his hearing had dimmed with the years. Each Sunday he took his place as Ordinary of the Chapel and on weekdays it was the rule of his life to be present at the head of table during the evening meal of the college. It was sometimes said that in his earlier days he had been a dangerous man to cross in argument or policy, but in age his character, if it had ever been uncharitable, had mellowed into a gracious willingness to concede the interest of other men's opinions.

I poured myself a glass of Madeira and sat down beside him.

"I always opposed those trees," he said. "Corinthian columns and foliage; Venus with a petticoat!"

The coals burned hot and red between the marble columns of the fireplace. I listened to Dr Ashton's slow, clear voice. His hands lay very still, crossed on his knees. His face was calm, almost expressionless.

27

"I put a curse on the birch nearest the chapel," he said quietly. "But it worked on the other one."

I did not feel it behoved me to say anything so I merely smiled. We sat quietly for a time. At length the others began to make their excuses and depart to their rooms, or to meetings, or home, only Dr Ashton, Lessop and I remaining.

"Would you have time for a game of chess?" I enquired.

"Just a quick one," said the Senior Fellow. "I have to walk home these evenings and I do not want to be late."

All summer Dr Ashton drove to and from the house where he lived alone, but his insurance company objected to him driving at night so in the winter he walked the two miles into college and returned on foot after dinner.

I set out the pieces and moved the chess table nearer to him.

"Will you take white?" he asked me.

I demurred at being given an advantage.

"You are right not to give yourself an excuse for losing" he said, and we put the matter to the decision of what men call chance. "So I am drawn to play against black," he continued as he saw the piece in my hand, "light against darkness."

He opened, pawn to king's four. As we played, Lessop, who was also a chess player of some distinction, divided his attention between our game and an article in the *Economist*.

Those of my listeners familiar with chess will perhaps be disappointed, those unfamiliar relieved, when I say that I will not, indeed I cannot, follow our game in detail to its conclusion. I could not recall it distinctly the next day, and time has done nothing to assist in the matter. But my impression is that I never succeeded in breaking the Reverend Doctor's pawn formation. I contrived two diverting and unorthodox attacks on his queen but each was effectively contained and I eventually lost both position and ground to him. Dr Ashton then brought two bishops and his queen into play and wrought such havoc behind my forward position that resignation appeared to be the only Christian virtue which the circumstances would permit.

"Yes," he agreed, "I would put little trust in your position: it can only grow worse, even fatal if you struggle. But thank you. It has been a good game. You are a promising player."

Outside the chapel clock struck nine. "I must go," he said. "What time was that?"

Both Lessop and I stood up as Dr Ashton took his leave of us. His tall, upright figure inspired me with an awe such as I have never experienced with any other man. His black gown hung straight down from his shoulders and he held his head with dignity and strength. I remember thinking as he left the room that what the years had taken away were merely the outward decorations, the feathers and gew-gaws of youth. The citadel of the man was unstormed, unshaken. He would meet death full front in battle. He would not be dragged down reluctantly, a fugitive in the night.

We sat down as the door closed behind him. Lessop, who had not spoken at all while we were playing, leaned forward and examined the board.

"You know you have given up far to easily. The old man has been deceiving you. You can perfectly well get out of that position. In fact," he added briskly, "I think you can win!"

"I don't see it," I said after examining the board for some moments.

"Very well, if you have time, move over to white and play out Ashton's position for him and I'll take your place."

I remember I made some show of an objection. The fire, hitherto almost too hot for comfort, had suddenly burned into white

29

ash and I was feeling a distinct chill in the room. However, Lessop seemed very keen and eventually I agreed to finish the game with him.

A chess board can look quite alarmingly different if one suddenly changes ends and I was at once aware that I had quite a different role to sustain. It had been black's move, and Lessop used it in a way which clearly impeded my inherited tactics. I sat back from the board and considered the situation at length. As far as I could see Dr Ashton, that is to say I, could checkmate in four moves provided black did not move his king in the next move. I advanced a pawn one square to begin the blockade. Lessop ignored what I had done and adjusted a castle one square to the side. It seemed a peculiarly footling move and it had, I thought, given the game to me. "Check!" I said, lining up a bishop on his king. Without hesitation he interposed a knight as I had expected him to do. I advanced my other bishop half way across the longest diagonal in the board. I anticipated that my next move with the same bishop could not be prevented, and would give me the game. "Mate!" said Lessop with finality and marked satisfaction as he brought his second knight to bear on my king. I had raised a hand to move the king before I saw to my dismay that every possibility was either blocked or covered. I have seldom been caught so unawares in a game. The thing was almost past belief. It was obvious when it was done; but I had had no apprehension of it.

"I'm sorry, Lessop," I said at length. "I think I've let Dr Ashton down rather badly. He never would have allowed this to happen to him."

"I'm afraid I disagree," remarked the botanist. "I think he foresaw perfectly well that defeat was inevitable, and he accepted that the game had beaten him even if his opponent didn't see how to follow out the moves."

"Was mate inevitable?" I asked doubtfully.

"Yes, given that black makes the moves you have seen. Set it up for yourself again and have a look."

"It seems rather odd to have put myself in a winning position against Dr Ashton and not known it," I remarked as I stood up from the table. "What kind of a player loses both sides of the same game!"

"Don't take it to heart," said Lessop half mockingly, "a man is often enough caught in a web he doesn't know he is weaving. But Ashton's a good player – at life as well as chess. Don't underestimate his foresight. He knew he would lose if you could have seen the real strength of your position. He just codded you into resignation. Good night to you."

The Senior Common Room door closed. I lit my pipe and sat down again in an easy chair with my back to the door and turned away from the chess table. I stretched my feet towards the embers of the fire. A faint warmth spoke of coals consumed but not quite dead. I was irritated with myself and out of humour with Lessop, nor could I keep Dr Ashton out of my mind. I felt I had let him down in some way; that I had exposed a weakness in him which had been legitimately concealed in perfectly straightforward play. To be candid, I did not like Lessop. He was an abrupt, ungracious man; far too young to have been made a professor and far too clever for the comfort of his colleagues. I remembered with displeasure the sharp way in which he had answered Ashton about the eucalyptus shrubs.

The room was very quiet as I sat there alone. I could hear the tick of the French clock over the fireplace. No sound from the world outside broke in upon the stillness. A coal in the fire shed its ash. I half closed my eyes and was for a moment strongly inclined to go to sleep. But I was obliged to do some work that evening and would have to go. I was about to set myself in motion when I remembered the Madeira which had stood untouched on the chess table during the interest of the two games. I half rose to fetch the glass and then held still in surprise. I can remember that surprise was at first my only reaction. Dr Ashton had returned and was sitting at the chess table about five yards away (metres as I must now say) with his back to me examining the board. I stood up and said something like: "I'm sorry, I hope you don't mind, but Lessop wanted to play out the game and I'm afraid I made a mess of your position."

Dr Ashton gave no indication of having heard me but continued his examination of the board. I have already said he was slightly deaf, and I was about to move forwards to repeat my apology in a louder voice when it occurred to me that, just as I had not heard him come in, so he had probably failed to notice me sitting in the armchair by the fire. I would probably startle him as well as upset his concentration if I suddenly intruded myself. Instead of speaking again I backed quietly away and sat down; this time on the opposite side of the fireplace so that I could see him, half back view, without having to turn round in my chair. He remained quite still for some time, as it seemed to me, and then adjusted a piece on the board. I assumed that his recollection of the state of the game must have worried him and that he had come back to examine it. I was heartily sorry we had moved the pieces, but if he had foreseen checkmate in his position he would have at once realized what had been done on the board. We remained thus for perhaps five minutes while all the time I became steadily more embarrassed. Having failed to speak when I first saw him I seemed to have lost all opportunity to speak at all, and I had no idea how I would explain my silent presence when he observed me. At length he lifted his head from the board and, although he was still three-quarters turned away from me, I heard him say slowly, "I hoped the combination of bishops might have succeeded, but now I see the game is indeed lost. The black knight is master of us all. I accept."

He stood up slowly, still with his back to me. As he did so, part of the sleeve, or possibly a fold in his gown seemed to catch in the table. He did not turn to unloose it so that as he walked towards the door most of the length of his gown swept across the table carrying all the pieces to the floor where they fell silently in the muffled stillness of the room. Apparently he did not notice for he neither turned nor hesitated. For a moment my eyes strayed to the fallen chessman and when I looked up he had gone.

The French clock gave one of its sharp pings like a tiny silver droplet falling into a crystal jar: a quarter to ten. I started to my feet as if from sleep, more than a little relieved at having avoided discovery. I picked the pieces off the floor and carefully put them away in the box. Then I looked at the table. The Madeira was still precisely as I had set it down when Dr Ashton and I began to play two hours earlier. It was full and unspilt while all the pieces on the board had been knocked down. I picked it up and drank it quickly. The improbability of the thing struck me at once, but it was not for another minute or so that I brought myself to acknowledge that my own eyes had seen Dr Ashton's gown draped *right over* the table and then pulled away carrying *all* the chess pieces to the floor. I set my empty glass back on the table and retreated from it. For the first and only time that evening I experienced the fluttering movement of feeling which is the beginning of fear. On the sideboard one of the candles went out with a hiss and I made sudden haste to leave the darkening room and the dead fire.

Once outside I felt neither alarm nor fear: only a vague and troubling sense that I had been the spectator of something which

I knew I ought not to have seen. I resolved never to mention the matter to Dr Ashton. I went straight to my rooms and tried to immerse myself in a study of Robertson's *Charles V*. But at length, unable to concentrate, I gave up and read a novel for an hour or two before going to bed where I slept very badly.

I was awakened unpleasantly at eight o'clock by Larry, my scout (administrative grade D as we call them now). He was in a cheerful humour and blurted out the day's news without preamble.

"Bad news," he said without any visible diminution of his early morning zest. "Old Dr Ashton was taken ill last night on his way home. Died before they could get him to hospital. Never regained consciousness they say."

I dressed as fast as I could and arrived at college breakfast in a sweat of impatience and apprehension. By the sort of merciful coincidence not often granted in life the next man down was Dr Todd, one of our Fellows in the School of Medicine, who seldom came in to breakfast.

"Yes, I was called," he said in answer to my question. "He collapsed at the Front Gate on his way out of college and the porter sent for me. Heart attack I am almost certain. He was still alive when I came but unconscious and failing fast. I stayed with him in the ambulance and did what I could, but a man of eighty-nine is already at the edge of life and there was no helping him. He was a fine man."

"When did he die?" I asked. Part of me did not want to know the answer.

"At exactly a quarter to ten by my watch. He rallied for a moment and seemed to think he was going home. I think he said, 'It's a dark night', or something like that. Then he died. It's not often death certificates can be made out so precisely," the doctor added with a touch of bitterness.

It was on the tip of my tongue to speak about the chess game but I hesitated. I could expect little but the scepticism with which I myself would have greeted a similar story. I resolved to keep my peace then, and I have never broken it since. But now the medical staff inform me that plant utilization directives oblige them to withdraw some of the aids to life which have kept my mind, if not much of my body, active these past two years. Thus I have at last dictated my account. It cannot matter now whether I am believed or not. It's hard to understand that Dr Ashton died only sixty years ago: too soon to take advantage of the earliest geriatric revivification units. No one is allowed to die like that now. Not now. Not until it is convenient.

Cropsey's Hole

These hills abound with precipitous rocks, caverns, and
water-falls, beside interminable morasses, full of deep
ruts, which are nevertheless often green and dry at the
bottom, with perhaps a small rill tinkling along each of
them. No superior hiding-place can be conceived.

The Brownie of Bodsbeck

Clever, rich and enviably well married, Adam Gray nevertheless
sat alone by the dying fire listening to the BBC amusing away
the last few minutes of the old year. Instead of the social hum of
the West London suburbs, a savage wind tore at the empty landscape outside. Instead of diversions and family, he was embroiled
with himself. It had been a bad mistake. His dark features – he
almost consciously cultivated their similarity to the conventional
stage image of Mephistopheles – were relaxed from the arrogant
and supercilious cast with which he was wont to disconcert hostile witnesses. The black hair, normally swept straight back from
the low line of the forehead, was ruffled by the perpetual fidget-

ing of his fingers. It had been a mistake, and now it was compounded by bad luck.

He had complained bitterly to Myriam, his wife, about staying with her mother yet again for the New Year. But it might be her last year with them. He had heard that before, and said so. His mother-in-law had all the physical indestructibility of the permanent invalid. As an overworked Queen's Counsel, his own hold on life could well be less secure. In a fit of simulated pique, contrived to make Myriam feel as if she were letting him down, he had driven himself to their small country house at Westwinds intent upon accepting a standing invitation from the Morwicks to join them for the New Year shooting. Myriam had promised to drive up after him on the second of January. But the Morwick household had been suddenly laid low by flu (or some such inconvenience) and the party was cancelled. So here he was, three hundred miles north of London, stuck with nothing worthwhile to do, and the only alternatives either admitting defeat to his wife, or returning alone to an empty house at Putney.

A wild rattle of sleet at the window drowned out the Third Programme for a moment, and broke through his self-absorption. Wind, always that damned wind blasting and tearing at the place! The wind figured less prominently in his memories. When he had first been there with his parents, and later with Tom Heathfield when they were both reading for the Bar, the winter days always seemed still and cold. Clear sunshine and long shadows across snow-covered hills where the Romans walked. That was what he remembered. He barely exchanged Christmas cards with Tom now: Tom with whom he had grown to manhood, talked, argued, rowed, tramped across the High Atlas, and in whose company he first met Myriam. It was such a pity that Tom had taken onto him as wife that plain, glum, jealous little woman called Sally, who had made it clear to Gray on his one and only visit that he was not welcome. But Adam knew that his disparaging thoughts were not quite honest. Sally was for him the inscrutable justice of things working itself out. She excluded him from the only man for whom he had ever felt real friendship, just as he had excluded Tom from the only woman Tom had ever genuinely loved. If only he had kept clear of the challenge, poor, drab, aggressive little Sally would never have appeared and Myriam would have been Tom's wife. If only ...

The Third Programme announcer was saying, "and finally part of the string quartet in D minor, 'Voces Intimae', to take us up to Big Ben and the New Year". Another gust of wind shook the casement. Myriam would almost certainly try to ring him after midnight. It would make her feel just that little bit more upset at abandoning him in favour of her mother if she couldn't get through. He walked out to the hall and took the receiver off the rest, placing it behind the curtain on the window sill. Nothing moved on the moorland road half a mile away, and neither of the distant hill farms showed a light. No one would first foot him. He was confident of that. They probably didn't even know he was there. He asked nothing from them; they took nothing from him. It was the way he liked it.

On his return to the study he picked up the sheaf of papers by a certain Will Turnbull which the village newsagent had pushed into his hand the previous day asking whether they were worth publishing as a local memoir. It was rough stuff – mostly about work at one of the small local coalmines that had all disappeared long since, and life in the village school in the 1920s – but some of it had a direct and vigorous interest. One paragraph caught Adam's attention:

One cave in particular stands out in my memory. We used to call it Cropsey's Hole. The entrance having slid or fallen and subsequently grown over with heather and bracken, provided a space which we could just manage to crawl through at that time. Once inside, the cave was about the size of a large room and at some time in the distant past had been provided with benches of granite or sandstone. I daresay the entrance will, over the years, have become completely hidden and much of the hill has since been planted by the Forestry Commission. I wonder if boys will again stumble on this cave.[†]

Now that was an idea which could occupy New Year's Day if the storm abated. Why not look for Cropsey's Hole? He had boots, tweeds, leggings: indeed everything for the purpose; and he and Tom had always had just such a walk in the old days.

He stood up to give the fire a final poke before going to bed. He loved fires and missed them in London. The hot coals glowed responsively and then dust and smoke blew into his face as a gust of wind sucked down the chimney. He started back, wiping his eyes and coughing.

*

"Yes, Bexhill 100227, Myriam Gray speaking." A hard female voice with a trace of the flat accent of Yorkshire was talking with anxious haste at the other end of the wire.

"O Sally! How nice to hear from you. We haven't met for *ages*. Happy New Year! ... No, we haven't gone to bed yet. Are you all right? ... What did you say? ... Tom? ... O no! ... When? ... Last night? ... O my dear, I'm *so* sorry ... No, I can't ... He's at Westwinds for the shooting and he's obviously got the receiver off the

---

[†]From *A Northumbrian*, an unpublished manuscript by a local person, probably from Ward's Hill, which came into the Author's possession some years ago under curious circumstances.

hook, I've tried to phone him several times since midnight ... Yes, I'm afraid it's the sort of thing he would do – he doesn't like New Years. But look, I'll send a telegram right away. I'm sure he'll come if Tom asked for him ... Yes, I suppose we always do ... Look, I'm coming north myself tomorrow ... yes I mean Tuesday, to join Adam. I'll call in on the way . . . Yes, the A1 is no distance ... No, *please* don't go to any trouble at all. I just thought it might be a way of joining up with Adam and perhaps seeing ... Yes ... Goodbye ... Be brave, Tom's a strong man. He'll pull through."

Myriam slowly put the receiver down and sat gazing for a moment into the past, her tall, thin figure braced against nothing on the telephone stool. It could so easily have been her at the other end of that call talking to someone else who would have been Adam's wife.

"Who was that dear?" Her mother's voice was diffident but emotionally demanding. It said to her, "I don't want to intrude dear, if you don't want to tell me, and I know I'm deaf, but ..."

"O ... er ... just Adam wishing us both a happy New Year."

She would send the telegram when her mother was safely tucked up in bed with her hot-water bottles. She did not want the painful questioning which might follow too much information about the state of affairs between her and Adam, and her mother's recollection of Tom would be even more intrusive. She could hear it already: "Such a nice boy. I remember your father thought he wasn't good enough for you. But I always liked him ..."

*

Adam rolled over in bed. The dim red electronic numerals of the radio alarm flicked on to 8.14 a.m. He had an uncertain sense that some familiar voice had called him as he woke, but the impression rapidly receded into the dream-depths of his consciousness. It was time to rise if he was to recreate the past, take a great New Year's Day walk, find Cropsey's Hole. The wind had ceased. Light, clear and still, suffused the sky behind the Alnwick moors. The ground was hard with a salting of hoar-frost at the roots of the grass. The walking would be perfect.

At ten o'clock he set out in brilliant sunshine encumbered by no more than the lightest of packs containing a large thermos of hot, sweet tea, some cold pork pie from Melton Mowbry, a bar of plain chocolate, and a miniature flask of Old Glenlivet. In a reluctant concession to possible visitors he pinned a brief note to the front door on his way out. "Back about 3 p.m. Out walking."

The first half mile was up a lane to the main road which ran north-south across the skirts of the hills. He crossed it quickly, the little haversack snug at his back. He was at the far side of the first sheep enclosure, a field of rough pasture more or less fenced off from the heather moor proper which lay beyond, before he remembered that he had not replaced the telephone receiver. It was a pity. He had a vague idea that putting it back would have confirmed to a caller that he was out rather than leaving things uncertain; but he would be back within four or five hours. It could scarcely matter much.

His immediate objective was the most southerly of the several named sites which he planned to investigate in looking for Cropsey's Hole. On the map it was marked as "Selby's Cove" and would take him nearest to the ugly blocks of spruce with which commercial afforestation had disfigured the hills towards Rothbury. He must have been there before, but he could not remember whether "cove" indicated a cave or, in the old style of the area, a stone hutment. From Selby's Cove, whatever it was, he proposed to turn north to the Ousen Stones on Swallow Knowe and then finally, if he had time, to look at Coe Crags.

By far his easiest course was to follow the Bracken Burn for about two miles. It kept almost all the way in a shallow depression dotted with rowans, stunted thorn, birch and scrub oak, and although following many small changes of direction of its own, its general drive was straight to his first objective. At the end it split into two, one runnel or "syke" continuing due west to Selby's Cove, the other, "Ousen Syke", turned north across a patch of mossy ground to rise near his second search area.

The walking was enjoyable, but he was compelled to stop more frequently than he wished where the land was rough or rising steeply. The social life had put him more out of condition than he suspected. He must try to get more regular exercise at home. For some time he walked on, his mind an agreeable blank. At the dividing of the stream he looked back, but he was now at the bottom of a steep cutting which the water had worn into the surface of the moor. It had a forbidding look, very still and in shadow. A curlew trilled somewhere out on the moor recalling him oddly to the moment of waking that morning. Then the call receded again. It was probably a subconscious guilt about Myriam. Blast Myriam! He wanted to enjoy the walk, not vex over the minor imperfections of his marriage. With a gesture of impatience he resumed walking towards Selby's Cove.

It was a hutment. The scatter of stones unmistakably indicated a long house: one of the earlier forms of habitation in the district. A ruined stell was situated to the west, presumably where Selby had penned his sheep or beasts. But the remains could scarcely conceal the refuge Turnbull had described.

The Ousen Stones were more promising. Why they were so named was unknown to him. They seemed to have no conspicuous significance, being merely several acres of sandstone outcrops, eroded into fantastic overhangs, or tumbled about in confused heaps of enormous boulders. Adam spent all of an hour wandering about in them like a fox in a megalithic graveyard. The place was full of shelters and short caves, but nothing corresponded to Turnbull's description of Cropsey's Hole, and nothing of more dramatic interest than the scattered horns, wool and bones of a dead sheep revealed itself. By half-past one he had had enough. The best of the day was past and the sun, never high at that season, was already sinking. He squatted down in the lee of a boulder to eat pie and sip hot tea. He smiled to himself. It was just the way he and Tom would have lunched. The smile faded, leaving him cold and full of years and unduly conscious of the pains and aches and limitations of his body. There had been no limitations then.

Half an hour later he stood up. Clouds were gathering quietly in the west. He must move. He was getting stiff and a bit cold. "Better be moving," Tom would have said. Like a boy showing off to an admiring friend, Adam jumped down off the ledge on which he was standing. It was a good jump, and he had to follow it out with two quick steps forward through the long stick heather. For a hideous instant he was trying to walk on empty air, then he was falling, clawing frantically at heather at his face. His fingernails tore at stone, his mouth smashed into something hard and dirty. With a shocking jolt his body scraped agonizingly between rocks and tumbled into darkness.

*

The realization that the old telegram service was no more had not dawned upon Myriam until her attempt to set a message on its way to Adam in the small hours of New Year's Day after her mother was in bed. She learned that if telephone contact could not be established, a telemessage, which she could dictate, would be given "hard copy" and delivered by first-class post on the first working day following receipt of the message. Since New Year's Day was a Bank Holiday, nothing could be delivered until Tuesday, January 2nd. That was the day that she was going north anyway. As a gesture she left a telemessage asking Adam to go to Tom's place near Harrogate, or at least phone Sally at once. It might help.

She eventually went to bed, angry with Adam, and angry with the Post Office. "What a wreck of an age to live in!" was almost her last thought as she fell asleep, to dream of Tom in agreeable fantasies which were always cut short with the empty awareness that something was not as it should be.

In the morning and throughout Monday she made attempts to phone Adam, eventually eliciting from the exchange the information of which she was already aware – that the receiver had been left off the hook. She contemplated phoning the Morwicks but dismissed the idea. They were ten miles away from Westwinds and Adam had let her know about the flu. In mid-afternoon she phoned Sally to admit her failure to contact Adam, and to ask about Tom. It was not good news. After being able to speak a little at first he had sunk into a deep coma following a second stroke. He remained unconscious. Myriam's words of conventional sympathy and reassurance uneasily covered her deeper concern.

Throughout the long day her anger at Adam's selfish isolation and her irritation with inactivity increased; irritation which found an object in her mother whom she twice reduced to tears, and once to announcing that she wished she was dead since she was just a nuisance to people now. In desperation, Myriam belatedly invented a telephone call from Sally in order to explain her excessively early departure the next morning.

"You were always very fond of Tom weren't you?" Her mother had at once remarked. The remark was innocent enough, but it made Myriam wince. She had to tell herself firmly that she loved her mother (which was true); but she was uncomfortably aware that her mother used the emotional flagellation of her New Year visit as a weapon to needle Adam, and that when things went wrong she ought to blame herself not the old lady. By the end of the day she hated everyone, even the TV weatherman who was promising snow in the north with some drifting and difficult travel conditions.

She packed her luggage before going to bed in the suffocatingly sealed-up heat which her mother always said she needed. She was worried and saddened. She ought to have gone that morning. But she hadn't thought about it properly, and doubted if she could have faced the "Well if you have to, then of course you must ... but I had hoped ... well never mind" sequence. Anyway it was too late now.

*

For a period Adam lay on his face, stunned by the abruptness of the calamity and the shock of physical injury. He must have fallen between two big rocks which had been hidden by the shaggy heather, but it had happened so quickly he was confused. His face was scraped in the fall, and he could feel blood running down his forehead. He had broken at least two front teeth, and his lips were cut. He was badly shaken and jarred all over. His left leg was beginning to hurt badly below the knee, and he was in near darkness. Tentatively he moved his right hand. All well. Then his left arm. All well again. Then his right leg. He wriggled his toes experimentally. Then he turned his investigation to his left leg. With great caution he braced the muscles to draw up his foot. The pain

45

did not sensibly increase. Probably nothing broken. His feet must have struck the bottom of the hole first, and then he must have crumpled up as they failed to take the weight of his body. He had suffered most of the damage at the top, and was now lying at the bottom of a cavity at least big enough for him not to be touching the sides anywhere.

Cautiously he raised his head and then braced his hands against the sandy floor to help him into a crouching position. He could see daylight directly above, raggedly meshed over by the roots and stems of heather. He could even see them stirring slightly in the wind, although at that moment he could hear no corresponding sound. Very carefully, feeling about as he did so, he stood up, ready at any moment to relax if his hands or head found an obstruction. Evidently he had broken no bones: scratches, a torn face, grazed fingers, and a bruised leg. He patted gingerly at his face with a handkerchief. It was shatteringly bad, but it could be worse.

Still without moving sideways, he looked up again at the chimney down which he had fallen. The light on the weathered rock was not good, but his eyes, always adept at night sight, were rapidly adjusting. The roof, where it turned upwards into the chimney, was about four feet above his head. He extended his arms towards the light, then sideways. Almost at once, and on both sides, he encountered the downward slope of the roof. He quested forward with a foot – more sand – and followed the roof down with his hands. The slope continued, and then turned down in a gently bulging wall which reached the ground about four feet from where he had fallen. With insignificant variations the same features were repeated behind him. The hole was thus nine or ten feet wide – or long – at the point where he had fallen. A similar, but much longer investigation conducted at ninety degrees to his first moves established that on one side the cavern terminated abruptly in what appeared to be a uniform stone wall, while in the other direction it continued for some distance – several yards anyway – as the roof and walls converged to what might or might not be an aperture in the pitch darkness. The ground was sandy, with here and there domes of flat sandstone apparent. At least there appeared to be nothing further to fall into. One other feature that Adam registered on his first investigations was that down the length of the cavern, on both sides, the walls formed deep ledges, like benches, before reaching the floor.

Adam thus formed a crude mental picture of his position. It was like being under an upturned boat. He could all too easily stand upright under the "stern" where he had fallen through, but how to climb back up again out of an upturned funnel was frighteningly uncertain.

What time was it? His watch was not luminous, but by stationing his wrist carefully beneath the chimney, and keeping his head back out of the light, he could just read the reflective surface of the hands. An hour had passed already. Something cold fell on the back of his hand. It turned to water as he touched it. Snow. So he was buried in Cropsey's Hole, or something very like it, with snow falling on the moor above and the nearest farm at least two miles away. Unless someone looked at his door after three that day, no one would realize that he had failed to return; and when Myriam did look tomorrow, late tomorrow, she would not know to which day "gone walking" referred. He had in fact disregarded every rule of good hill craft. He had told no one where he was going, had carried no emergency rations, no matches, no torch, not even a bright coloured piece of clothing, which might help searchers to find him. For a while he experienced a numb and black despair which rapidly gave way to a stunning fear. He was going to die.

47

A few minutes later he had mastered himself again. He was going to survive the night, and in the light of morning he would see what could be done. If this *was* Cropsey's Hole, then there was some way in or out, presumably without falling ten feet or using a rope. He sat down on the ledge by one of the walls. What had he got? Gloves, haversack with a spare pullover in it, half-full thermos, untouched whisky, half a bar of chocolate, key, useless money, a very thin waterproof anorak, hat – hat! He had been wearing one when he fell. For some time he groped about the floor below the almost extinct light of the chimney, but without success. He was about to give up when his fingers encountered a small, damp lump of ... of cloth. He hastily dropped whatever it was, and groped his way back to the stone bench, but more confidently now. No bad thing really if anyone should be looking for him for his hat to have been left outside on the heath.

The sense of business and self-reliance and things to do, or think about, or investigate with his hands: all helped to keep his imagination at bay. Turnbull had written about a bench with room for a dozen or more men to sit in comfort. Gray explored sideways with his hand. The bench was undoubtedly natural whatever Turnbull might have thought. The slight ribbing and the rounded edges were never masons' work. Cautiously he made his way along until his head came into contact with the roof. Stooping lower he continued until he could go no farther without having to get down flat on his stomach. The ledge, roof, and floor converged. Discouraged, he returned to his starting point and then moved across to the other side to undertake the same investigation.

The result was very similar although the shelf was deeper. He was about to give up when his questioning fingers touched something which was not rock. For a second he drew back in apprehension and then felt towards it again. It was woody, soft: lots of little twigs and branches compressed together like a pad, and quite extensive; a large mass of very dry, flattened heather – unmistakably heather – a sort of bed lying loose on the rock. It was the first faint promise, if not of hope, at least of an alleviation of discomfort. This was no accident. It was the work of man, and served to confirm his suspicion. He was in Cropsey's Hole. Still moving carefully in the darkness, he shifted his haversack and gloves across to the heather couch. He was consciously trying to act out the situation with maximum intelligence and judgment as if he were trying to satisfy a critical and friendly observer. It was a helpful fiction, and given the area, quite natural to suppose that Tom was watching him.

There was one aspect of his prison to which he had as yet given no attention – the walls: the areas between the roof and the ledges. Working now with elaborate thoroughness, he felt his way round. They were generally without distinctive features but gave way here and there into small cup holes, wind or water eroded at some much earlier period when the boulder must have been exposed. One or two contained sand. In one he found water. He was about to give up when his fingers found a ledge in the rock almost where he had started: at the bed's head as it were. On it was something smooth. Wax! A candle! Unmistakably a candle, about four inches long and quite fat but apparently without a wick. Guttering still sealed it to the rock, but the shelf went deeper. His searching fingers followed it. They were grazed and cold, but still with feeling enough to discern shapes and textures. Merciful heaven, there was a little soft box there!

He picked it up with an almost comic combination of eagerness and care. It shook. There were matches in it, but the box was soft and damp and it took a great deal of patience to open it without breaking the box or spilling the contents. He felt the matches.

49

The heads were intact. There was no evidence of that confusing habit of putting the burnt ones back with the living for tidiness or from whatever motive. But they were soft. Laying them aside for a moment he put on the spare pullover from the haversack and carefully tucked it inside his belt. Then he sprinkled a number of the precious matches in between his shirt and the two pullovers he was now wearing. With luck the warmth of his body would dry them somewhat, and for the final heat up he would employ the hot tea which still remained in the flask. It was just a matter of waiting until impatience or the cold drove him into action. He pulled on the woollen gloves rather painfully, squashing the haversack into a semblance of a pillow and lay down on his back on the heather couch.

With the complete darkness and the cessation of activity the enormity of what had happened returned more powerfully to his attention. He was entombed in a hillside beneath a snowstorm, his face and hands were sore, his teeth ached unmercifully, and his left leg was stiff with what must be a nasty bruise. He could hear the wind breathing remotely but none of it seemed to find its way into the cavern. A long time passed. His imagination took him elsewhere and he followed the possibilities of an important case in his mind. Then the cold began to intrude again. It clung to him like a shroud, particularly to his legs. Why? Because there must be some slight movement of air taking place in the lower end of the cavern where floor and roof converged, and which he could not investigate without light.

He sat up stiffly and fumbled for the clean, dry paper handkerchief which remained in his breast pocket. Folding it out flat on his knees, he emptied the matches onto it from inside his jersey. Several were probably lost, but the majority remained safely. The heads were certainly firmer than they had been. Next he folded them up in the tissue, and placed it on his knee again before emptying hot tea from the thermos into its cup. With great care he picked up the pad of matches and clamped it to the bottom of the hot mug and waited. Every few moments he sipped at the wonderfully hot sweet liquid. The matches were becoming very satisfactorily warm. He prayed they were not the safety variety; for the box (whose shape suggested Swan Vestas) was too soft and damp ever to provide a robust enough abrasive.

O damn! He had forgotten to pare down the candle to find its wick. He groped in his pocket for the miniature silver pen-knife he always carried, and turned awkwardly to scrape at the candle on its ledge behind him. The job was easily done, and he could soon feel the wick between forefinger and thumb. With relief he turned back, catching the cup as he did so with his sleeve. With a cry of anguish his hand slapped down on his knee to save the matches, but they had gone with the cup. The floor – quickly – they mustn't get damp. He was down on his hands and knees feeling about in frantic haste. They mustn't get damp. The tissue had fluttered open. Here was one, and another. Where were they all? There must have been fifteen or more. They must have flown away in the dark. It must be done quickly. If he could light one he might save the others. Pressing his finger hard against the head, he scuffed it across the sandstone. A line of tiny points of blue fire filled him for a moment with hope, but that was all. He tried again, and again, until the head was worn off the match. With the second one he tried another method. Instead of the single stroke from left to right, he rubbed it back and forward vigorously and continually in one place. He could feel the heat beneath his finger, then, with a minute explosion, there was fire.

Frantically, he applied it to the candle. My god it wasn't going to light! With his free hand he tore up a bit of the bedding and applied it to the expiring match. It took instantly. Half blinded by the flame he thrust it onto the candle. With much hissing and spluttering from its damp wick, the candle ignited. He flung the handful of burning heather onto the floor and for a few moments the cave was brilliantly lit with yellow fire. He grasped up the spilt matches which were now visible and slipped them into the breast pocket of his shirt. The heather burnt out leaving a sweet-smelling smoke behind.

Conscious of the need to conserve the candle, Adam looked round his prison. Its dark sandstone confines were uninteresting except for ancient initials burnt onto the roof with candle smoke – boys' work probably. There were several corners and crevices he had missed earlier, but all far too small to use even if they led any-where. The one exception was at the back were the two roof boul-ders sloped down into a low black aperture. The temptation was to look there and then, but Adam resisted it. If it were a way out there was at present no external light to guide him, and if he got out it would be into snow on a pitch-black moor. Better off where he was. He looked at his watch, with an awful realization that it was only seven o'clock. There would be at least twelve more hours of darkness, but there was little he could do except arrange his scanty possessions on the stone shelf by the candle. As a last pre-caution he warmed some of the remaining matches by holding them close to the side of the candle flame, and then stowed them with the others inside his breast pocket. Finally he wrapped the anorak round his legs and blew out the candle. The darkness could be endured. He was more apprehensive about the cold.

It is difficult to comprehend the extremity of chill and misery and aching discomfort to which an unprepared middle-aged man can be subjected by a night entombed in cold rock on the side of a bare mountain. Adam's shoulders pained him unmercifully, every position agonized him, his broken teeth and swollen lips ached, and the cold crept into his marrow so that he stiffened all over with a dreadful sense of immovable ague. At some stage he put his head inside the empty haversack in an attempt to keep the cold from his face and head, and in that position he may have slept until a voice spoke his name.

It was not clear to him how he could see the familiar figure sitting on the stone bench opposite. But he smiled without surprise.

I've been expecting you all day, he thought. I'm so glad you came after me. I've had rather bad luck.

It was a great comfort to have him there, and it was not in the least strange to find that Tom still retained the boyish handsomeness which had first captivated Myriam and which he had so unutterably envied.

"Tom." – the words he had never spoken flowed without reserve. "Tom, I know you loved Myriam, and I know you met her first. You challenged me. It was too easy for you. You made me try to interest her. But she didn't love you enough. Sally loves you much more than she did. But I'm sorry. It could have been different."

You did not take her. She took herself. I watched you both. But she never loved you. You interested her. You still do.

"I have fallen, Tom. What shall we do?"

We shall do nothing. We shall sleep.

Adam lay back on the couch, curiously light upon all the points of pain, and listened to the slow breathing of his friend who would be there to help him out of the pit when the time came.

"How shall we climb that chimney?"

There is no way to climb out Adam, but I will show you an easier way.

53

Adam almost consciously sank more deeply into the coma of sleep, drifting away from life down the long corridors and silent labyrinths of the world. He lay still and quiet. When he opened his eyes again there was no light. At first he could not understand where he was or what was missing. Then remembrance came back to him.

"Tom?" he said.

But the darkness gave back no reply. Slowly he recalled his desperate position, his discomfort, that he was so stiff he could scarcely move; that he was deadly cold.

He ungloved his hands carefully to avoid tearing the cuts on his fingers and felt numbly for a match. It lit quite easily this time, and so did the candle. He looked at his watch. To his confusion and horror it still said seven o'clock. It must have stopped. No, it was going perfectly and was sufficiently wound. Could it be 7 a.m.? It *must* be; it *had* to be. He had been unconscious, but things had happened in that unconscious which occupied time. It *must* be morning.

*

Myriam intended to leave while it was still dark on the Tuesday. Accordingly she went to bed early the previous evening, beseeching her mother as she did so not to try to get up to see her off but to wait in bed for the home help to arrive at nine. Perhaps she would. She would see how she felt. "Have a good night's sleep, dear."

Myriam did not sleep well. Her annoyance with Adam was beginning to be flecked with an ill-defined apprehension. He was a petty, vindictive brute when he was crossed, but he was not a fool. He would hurt her, not give her real grounds for suspecting that something was wrong if it was not wrong. And dear, kind Tom, dear Tom whose powerful kindly body she loved but whose colourless, pedestrian mind would have bored her to extinction within a few months of marriage: it seemed inconceivable that such a man could suddenly be near to death. She could not take her thoughts away from Tom. Had he understood? She had never dared ask and now she never could. The thoughts jumbled, criss-crossed, dissipated, and merged into the thin, black figure of her mother walking towards her across a landscape of dry volcanic ash, holding out to her a knife which was running with blood. Myriam would have turned away but Adam and Tom were writhing in the dust at her feet, their mouths and eyes stopped up with the stuff so that they clung to each other and to her without seeing their mortal danger from the knife. She tried to cover them, but fell into the choking debris herself. A shrill scream of terror resolved itself into the alarm clock. It took her several moments to grasp that it was Tuesday morning; that it was time to get going.

She rose, tired, unrefreshed, and ill at ease. Her mother was already up, groaning with just sufficient intensity to draw attention to her futile attempts to get a stocking onto her arthritic leg and yet allow her to reject help once the job was done: "There was no need to rush at it like that. I was managing. Now you've hurt my foot."

*

Adam edged himself upright, painfully, slowly. The dregs of the tea – the chocolate – a little whisky; that was the sum of his reserves. He poured the almost cold remains of the thermos straight into his mouth, alternating it with minute sips of the Glenlivet scarcely swallowed before it vapourized in his mouth to convey an illusion of warmth. The chocolate could be kept in reserve. Now move. Exercise gently in the widest, highest place under the chimney. Beat the arms. Try to walk on the spot. Breathe deeply. The last thought was almost put into his mind by ... he listened carefully ... no, it was impossible, just the wind.

As he exercised in an attempt to restore circulation to his numb extremities, the patch of sky above his head turned to dark blue, then lighter, then became suffused with pale yellow. It would be the full light of what promised to be a brilliant day by nine o'clock, and the day would last about six hours. If anyone were to come, they would come then. If he were to get out, it must be in those hours.

His first task was to use the candle to investigate the low end of the cave. It was evident from the slope of the flame that air was moving in from that end. He got down on hands and knees, and then flat on his stomach so that he could only wriggle forward like an arthritic snake. The cave continued, about two feet wide and eighteen inches high. It was a possible way. Moving the candle ahead of him step at a time, and then wriggling after it, Adam progressed about his own length, then halted, exhausted and defeated. It had indeed been a way. But now it ended in a tumble of stones which had been set, of all things, in concrete. Someone, sometime, had deliberately sealed off Cropsey's Hole.

Adam lay still for a few minutes, sick with disappointment and renewed fear. He was going to die there. The thought flashed across his mind. He thrust it aside. There was another way, there *must* be. It was too absurd to be helplessly entombed within a few miles of hundreds of people. He worked himself slowly backwards and then extinguished the candle to allow his eyes to become accustomed to the light that was now filtering down the chimney.

The first problem was how to attract attention. While eating lunch yesterday he had observed that the broad sweep of the hills allowed him an uninterrupted view down, across a length of the main road, and on almost to Westwinds. This meant that the precise aspect of the hills where he was trapped would itself be directly visible to anyone on or near the road, and a signal might be seen. He wouldn't suffocate with a fire if he retreated into the end he had just investigated, and the materials for a fire were at hand in the bed. A handful at a time, he transferred some of the finer, powdery bits to below the chimney, compressed it with his foot to encourage smoke rather than flame, and retrieved the old mildewed beret which he had touched the previous night. It would act as a damper. This done he settled himself to wait the short time until nine o'clock when it would be reasonable to expect people to be fully alive with the business of the day. He had sufficient matches to repeat the signal on the hour, every hour, whatever else he might do.

*

A red Land-Rover moved confidently along the main road. Jeff was not sorry to be on the move again after the New Year festivities.

Gawd what a night it had been! His head still ached slightly and the brightness everywhere after the light fall of snow didn't help. He turned down the lane to his last delivery. Not really much that morning for anyone. Business hadn't got started again. At the end of the lane to Westwinds he turned the van and picked up the last envelope, a telemessage for Mr Gray. Greetings probably. No one was up, at least no one was out. An untrodden sheet of snow about two inches deep covered the path to the front door. There had been no wind in the night worth mentioning and the stuff had flopped down equally over everything. As he slipped the envelope through the box he read the note, "Back about 3 p.m. Out walking." No one had been out walking that day. He knocked. No answer. He tried the door. Locked. With the curiosity and something of the neighbourliness of a countryman he made his way round the back of the house. His were the first footprints anywhere. He was not really alarmed, but it was peculiar, not quite right. He knew Mr Gray was supposed to be there, and he retained an affection for the family out of respect for old Dr Gray who had ushered him into the world sixty years earlier.

As he drove back up the lane towards the high road he decided to report the matter when he got back. His eyes scanned the hills casually. As he turned away to the left, a small quantity of brown smoke drifted up into the clear air about three miles away up on the whitened slopes. It was visible for a few minutes. But Jeff had his eyes on the road again and did not look.

*

Myriam was later than she intended in leaving her mother's house at Bexhill, but she was on the road by eight o'clock, which was good when she thought of all the possibilities of delay. She had made one final attempt to phone Adam before leaving and her failure yet again to get through had goaded her to hurry. She was glad she had bothered with the telemessage, and in her mind's eye she could see Sammy or Jeff delivering it to him.

By ten o'clock she was north of London, and at lunchtime she was looking for the Harrogate signs on the A1. Tom's house was a large Victorian villa on the east side of the town. she arrived at five minutes to two, just as Sally turned into the drive from the opposite direction with some shopping.

*

"Bell."

"Yes, sir?"

"We've just had a report in from one of the up-country post-men, Jeffrey Slater, do you know him?"

The constable shook his head.

"Well never mind. He reports from up Thrunton way that there's a note on a door, Adam Gray QC's door to be precise, at Westwinds, which leads him to suspect that someone, probably Mr Gray himself, went out for a walk yesterday or some time earlier and hasn't come back. We don't want any more unsolved disappearances in that district after the abandoned tent affair – that was before your time – so I spoke to Jeff myself after the report came in. We *may* have an emergency search on our hands. But first I want you to phone Gray's number here and at any other location you can find. I believe he has a house somewhere in London, and try his chambers too. I want to know if he's supposed to be up here still. Got it?"

"Yes, sir."

"Right. And in the meantime send a car to his house to check up. Tell them to report back here immediately, and then patrol the A697 in the vicinity until they get further instructions."

Constable William Bell was new to the force but highly intelligent and enterprising. He first tried the number for Westwinds and then, finding it engaged, instructed the exchange to check it out while a search was made for Gray's other locations. He had just found them when the message came back from the exchange that the phone was off the hook. The operator remembered doing the same test for someone, a woman she thought, the previous day.

Bell immediately put through a call to Putney. After a few

59

crackles a recorded message on an answerphone invited him to leave a message or, if Mrs Gray personally was wanted, to dial Bexhill 100227. The call to Bexhill was a long time being answered, and then a querulous voice said: "I'm very deaf. You must speak slowly and clearly."

"May I speak to Mrs Gray?"

"Yes."

"Do you want to speak to her?"

"Yes please."

"She's not here."

"Is Mr Gray there?"

"No, he's in Northumberland, shooting or something."

"Where is Mrs Gray now?"

"She's on her way to see him. Who is speaking please?"

Bell was vexed with himself. He had the idea he should have conveyed that information earlier.

"This is the police at Alnwick. We have reason to believe Mr Gray may have got into difficulties out walking, and we were wondering if Mrs Gray had heard from him recently."

"No. He wasn't out stalking; *shooting*, with friends called Moorcock or something. But he's quite all right. He phoned us yesterday.

"What time?"

"Late in the evening, to wish us a happy New Year."

"Are you quite certain?"

"Yes of course. Myriam, my daughter, Mrs Gray that is, told me quite clearly."

"Thank you Mrs er ... you have been most helpful. Do you know if Mrs Gray intended to get here today?"

"O yes. She left very early. About eight I think. She was calling at a friend's at Harrogate, someone very ill you know, such a nice boy."

"Do you know the name of the people she was calling on?"

"O yes. Tom. Tom Heathfield."

"Do you know his telephone number?"

"I don't think so."

"Never mind I can look it up. Could I just have a note of your own name?"

"Heathfield, H-e-a-t-h-f-i-e-l-d."

"No, *your* name."

"Mrs Cosby."

"Many thanks Mrs Cosby. You've been most helpful. We'll let you know if we have any news."

As she put down the receiver, Mrs Cosby smiled a private, inward smile. She had never liked Adam. Those nasty cold eyes! And it was exactly what Myriam had told her. But Constable Bell could not see Mrs Cosby's smile.

He looked at his watch. It was half-past twelve. The man's telephone had been off the hook long enough to provoke someone yesterday to ask the exchange to investigate, and it was off the hook now, and yet his wife had received phoned greetings from him late yesterday ... from somewhere. It did not feel quite right, but perhaps it was not far enough wrong to constitute an emergency. At least he could phone the Heathfield number although quite probably Mrs Gray would not arrive until ... maybe two o'clock. When he found the number, there was no reply. He would try later.

With that thought Bell reported back to his inspector, who had already had a telephone report in from the patrol car to the effect that, apart from desertion, the telephone visibly off the hook, and the inconsistency between the note on the door and the lack of any footprints except the postman's, all was in order. The inspector considered for a few moments, imagined various

61

trains of action, looked at his watch and came to a decision.

"Bell, if you were a good hill walker, and you were starting from the A697 between, say, New Moor House and Thrunton, where would you go?"

"Tor Crag or somewhere up there."

"I agree. Ask the car to keep in that general area until they receive further instructions. Tell them to keep a good watch on the hills. Put out a preliminary warning for a possible search, and alert Air-Sea Rescue to the possibility of a pick up in the general area of Rothbury Forest later today, and keep phoning that Harrogate number until you catch Mrs Gray. She may be able to let us all off the hook. Move!"

*

When he lit the first heap of finely crushed heather, Adam had been prepared to retreat to the back of the cave for air, but there was no need. The smoke rose straight up – not all that much of it for the heather was too dry – and disappeared out of the chimney. Within five minutes it was out. Adam resolved to repeat the signal every hour or so until darkness came. In an attempt to dampen some of the heather to increase the smoke, he scuffed some into the trace of snow which had fallen through during the night, and then turned his attention to a thorough examination of the chimney.

It was entirely inaccessible from where he stood, but with the farthest stretch of his fingers he could just touch the stone where it receded out of reach up the last three or four feet of vertical shoot. This in turn ended in a tangle of heather beyond which he could see the sky. The aperture was not round but elongated, like partly opened lips. The comparison was made more apt by a tongue of stone, some sort of flattish boulder he thought, sticking out into one corner of the mouth. The aperture was at most four feet long, at its widest two feet; one end vanished to a narrow wedge of light, the other was stopped open by the boulder. It was that, if anything, which offered a faint chance.

Adam gazed up until his neck ached and his eyes had almost lost the night vision necessary to operate in the cave. If only he had a grapple of some kind and a rope: something to catch in the jam of stone at the side of the tongue! He had his clothes, the haversack, the thermos, and the tiny antique pen-knife which had already been so useful. An idea was developing in his mind, and it could work. Anyway it was worth trying, and it was activity to a purpose, not just freezing and waiting for help that might not come. Between the smoke signals and his own efforts he would get out. He *would* get out!

He first turned his attention to the thermos, unscrewing its retaining top and extracting the silvered-glass thermos unit itself. What remained was a stainless-steel cylinder about a foot long and unusually strong: it was the sort of small personal item which Gray always bought expensively. With care and without haste he set about filling it with the silver sand which he could scrape up from the floor. When it was tightly packed, he screwed the cup back on and weighed the result in his hand with satisfaction. It was a bit heavy, but it could be lobbed up the chimney if he was careful, and its dense packing would keep it rigid; at least less liable to crush with the pull of the rope which was his next task.

Apart from attachment to the thermos, the rope would have to be at least six feet long, seven for preference, if he were to get a safe grip on it as it dangled back down the hole. He first dismantled the haversack, removed all the straps, and cut the stitches which bound the stout canvas sides and top together. One of the straps would make the attachment onto the thermos: that was a useful refinement he hadn't initially thought of. Then came the slow bit – slicing the canvas into inch-wide strips, being careful to avoid cutting into the strands running lengthwise along the strips.

Adam peered at his watch. It was already 11 a.m. Fire again! The ritual complete, he resumed his task. He had still his tie and belt, and strips could be made out of the back of his Norfolk jacket and plaited for strength. It would take time to get everything ready and safe, but he had time enough, and it was going to be done, it was going to be all right. "Tom," he suddenly said aloud, "I don't know what your easy way was, but I'm going to get out, boy. I'm getting out!"

*

Sally always looked glum and hostile, like a defensive child Myriam thought. But now she looked desperately tired as well. She had been out getting some shopping and had called in briefly at the hospital after spending all night there. Tom was in a deep coma after a second massive cerebral haemorrhage. There was nothing they could do. The two women walked towards the house. Had a phone call or a message come in from Adam? Myriam asked as soon as she decently could. No, but the phone had woken Sally at about one o'clock that morning as she dozed in the kitchen after the sleepless night, but it had stopped ringing before she could get to it. Since then she had been out. As they entered the house the phone started to ring again. Sally answered it.

"Sally Heathfield speaking ... You want Mrs Gray? Hang on, she's here. She's just arrived."

"It's for you," she said, her hand over the mouthpiece. "It's the police at Alnwick."

Myriam's heart gave an unpleasant bound as she took the instrument. The presage of disaster was overwhelming.

"Yes, Myriam Gray speaking ... Yes, this morning, I've just arrived. I hoped to see my husband here ... No, I haven't spoken to him since – since December 30th ... O did she? ... Yes, I'm afraid I led her to think he had phoned. I didn't want her worrying ... No, I've been frantically trying to get through to him since yesterday morning. I was just about to try again. What's the matter? ... I see ... Yes ...Yes. of course you can. Get in at once. Do anything you like ... I'll be at Westwinds in about three hours I suppose ... Yes, I'll be here until about three o'clock ... Thank you ... Goodbye."

She put the receiver down. Sally was unpacking listlessly in the kitchen.

"I'm afraid Adam's missing," she said. "The police think he's out on the moors somewhere. There's snow forecast."

It was a peculiar thing, but for a moment she thought she saw Sally's face lighten, then the shutters of grief came down again.

"Do you want to see Tom before you go on?" was all she said.

"Just for a few moments. It's been a long time. You don't need to come if you'd rather not. You look desperately tired."

"A'll cum. He's all I have. You've had children."

"They've grown up now."

"But you had them."

*

"That's it! Unless he's done a bunk he's somewhere out there." The inspector received Bell's report of his conversation with Mrs Gray as the decisive factor.

"Get onto the radio car and tell them to enter Gray's house, doing as little damage as possible, and report anything helpful back here at once. When you've done that, ask the local farmers – Fenmore, Cockershaws and Debonshiels for a start – if they saw anyone walking in the area on December 31st or January 1st. We've only got at most two hours of decent light and I wouldn't give much for his chances if we don't find him in that time, assuming he's still alive."

Within five minutes the radio report was back from the car: nothing disturbed, nothing out of the ordinary except the telephone off the hook, not a sign of anyone, although the house was obviously lived in. One of the men had found a piece of paper on the kitchen table which he thought might be helpful. It was a typed sheet with a paragraph describing Cropsey's Hole underlined in pencil.

"What the devil's Cropsey's Hole?" the inspector wanted to know. Constable Bell had already asked the same question and had the answer.

"It's a concealed cave, sir, some three miles south-west of Thrunton. Constable Milburn in the car knows exactly where it is. He used to go up there as a boy until his dad and some of the other farmers sealed it up because they thought it was dangerous."

"Could he still locate it?"

"Yes, sir."

"Could he find it from a helicopter?"

"I asked him that. He says he could. It's up the Ousen Stones on Swallow Knowe and he knows the land well enough to go straight there."

"Right, tell him to wait at Windysteads until a chopper picks him up, and then go straight to Cropsey's Hole and begin a search. Baylis, will you alert Air-Sea Rescue to the situation, ask them to pick up Milburn and fly on ahead. Also get a party to set out on foot with back-up equipment. Get a dog out there as well."

"Yes Bewick?"

"A report from Coe Farm just come in, sir. About an hour ago someone saw a small column of smoke over Swallow Knowe. They thought it unusual and reported it."

"That's him – it must be. Bell, we've got him. He's there *and he's alive*."

*

The short drive to the hospital where Tom lay were the worst minutes of Myriam's life. The two women travelled together in Sally's car in silence. That was uncomfortable enough, but her own feelings were in a cramped paroxysm of anguish: acute apprehension for Adam and his safety, sympathy for Sally, and a complete inability to know what her own reactions would be when she saw Tom.

He lay on his back in a room by himself, his face perfectly clear and untroubled, his eyes closed. His breathing was regular but shallow. Myriam bent over him. The face was uncannily, extraordinarily similar to her picture of twenty years ago and showed almost nothing of the harshness of the years. There still were the strong features, the firm jaw, almost the bloom of youth still on his skin. There, precisely, was the man she had rejected. She drew back for Sally. No tears would come now. It was a window strangely opened onto her past, and life had moved on. But it hurt. It hurt desperately.

Sally was bending over him.

"He's dying," she said simply.

Myriam watched, all her feelings arrested and put into a timeless suspense by the quiet mystery of the receding seconds. His breath was indeed coming more and more slowly and even as they listened it became less and less. Then, with a brief muscular spasm, the lips were drawn back in the vivid semblance of a smile, revealing for the last time to both women the beautifully regular teeth with which nature had endowed him at the beginning. After a long outgoing of breath, his face settled into the relaxed and youthful mask of death. Sally bent over him. Myriam turned away, a curious feeling of numbness inside her head as if she had just at that moment received a blow which had not yet begun to hurt. But the irony struck her absurdly; death apart, he was probably by far the healthiest man in the hospital. It was grotesque that such a man should be dead. *Grotesque!*

"Shall I call a nurse?" she asked quietly.

"No. I'll tell them on the way out. Man's aid can do no more for him – nor woman's neither."

"May I take you home?"

"Do as you wish. You'll have to pick up your car anyway, and you can phone Alnwick to find out if they have any news of Adam."

*

It took Adam longer than he had expected to strip part of his coat into bands of tweed, plait them, tie them economically to the straps and cut lengths of the haversack, plait in his tie and make optimum use of his belt in extending the length of the rope. He interrupted himself twice to light smoke signals and once to eat the last remains of chocolate, but by two o'clock the rope was ready to his best satisfaction, and secured firmly to the middle of the packed metal cylinder that had been his thermos flask.

The last stage would require a skilful throw and a lot of good luck, and he mentally prepared himself for a run of failures. His object was to lob the metal canister up into the corner of the chimney (where the tongue of stone protruded) in such a way that it would form a grapple by jamming in above the stone with the rope hanging out underneath, preferably in a corner.

In order to forestall the results of a bad throw which might result in canister, rope and all flying up through the hole out of reach, he unthreaded his boot laces, tied them together, attached one end to the end of the rope and the other to his left wrist. Then he stationed himself under the chimney, facing the corner where the tongue of stone protruded, but backwards from it. With great care he balanced the heavy canister in his right hand, measured with his eye the distance up into the dark aperture which must surely lie above the protruding stone, and lobbed the canister upwards. To his unrestrained delight it sailed upwards in a perfectly judged parabola and disappeared over and behind the stone tongue. He heard a satisfying clunk as the canister landed out of sight and a further movement as it adjusted its position somewhere behind the rock. The rope protruded over the tip of the stone and ended just in front of his face. As he tried a very delicate pull, he braced himself to catch the canister as it came back over the edge. But it did not come. Instead about four more inches of loose rope came free and he was able to flip the rope round the tip of the stone tongue into the corner so that it was in an ideal position to jam between the main boulder forming the side of the chimney and the corner of the tongue.

It was almost exactly what he had imagined to be possible, almost too good to be true. He increased his pull on the rope. It stretched a little as the knots tightened but that was all. Cautiously he allowed the rope to take more and more of his weight. Again it stretched, but nothing else moved or gave way. Finally he took his feet off the ground and hung by his hands, then jerked himself up one pull. Everything held. He dropped back to his feet, invigorated by the unexpected ease and speed with which his plan had worked.

Again he looked at his watch. It was just ten minutes past two. There was nothing to be gained by delay, but he was not quite ready for the final effort which he knew would test his weakened, out-of-condition muscles to the last scruple of endurance. There were his boots to re-lace, and he had to empty his bladder. It was curious how he had not thought of doing so before, but now he was bursting. With an irrelevant conventionality he took himself into a corner. Now there was a little ritual preparation for the climb which might help. He rather self-consciously worked his arms and legs in the best exercise he could devise to get the blood moving without risking cramp. He then drank the remains of the miniature Glenlivet on the half rationale that a little spirit would act as a cardiovascular dilatant, and that for a few desperate minutes this might be no bad thing. Finally, as if acting out the instructions of a rowing coach many years before, he began to take a succession of deep breaths quickly to "store up oxygen". When he stopped after twenty breaths, his heart was beating vigorously and he could almost feel the old challenge. He pushed his gloves in his pocket, buttoned his jacket, tensed and sprang at the rope.

The first few ascensions of hand over hand were comparatively easy despite the dead weight of his body. His hands were already up in the chimney but he could get no help from the rock until his head and shoulders were up there as well. His legs still dangled uselessly beyond the end of the rope. Up one. Up another. His hands and shoulders were screaming at him in agony already, but he would not let go. Up one. Up another. The blood pumped in his ears. In a curiously detached way he heard it as someone breathing beside him. Up another. His head was now up by the tongue of stone and he managed to grip the bottom of the rope with his feet so that the weight on his hands was slightly eased. Up one more. A hand on the tongue of stone. It was flat and went straight back out of sight just above his face. My god his left hand was slipping. With a frantic twist which defied all the probabilities of mechanics, he relieved his tearing left hand by wedging his right elbow over the top of the stone. For a moment or two he hung there, half broken with pain and exhaustion, half exhilarated with the relief of partial rest and the renewal of hope. His face was pressed awkwardly against the rock with his head twisted away from the shelf over which he had got his elbow, and it was not immediately possible to lean back far enough to turn his head the other way. His left hand had now to find a hold in the heather roots and wiry stems which reached down to him. Bracing his feet against the knotty rope, he found it. It held. The gasping, beating breath was still in his ears, but he was all right. This would show him! With a final convulsive effort he sliced his right hand out and over the stone shelf, straight into a ridge of something hard and sharp which was less solid and somehow more specific in contour than stone could be. Despite his precarious position he was now able to see what lay above the stone. Not twenty inches from his face two rows of fully exposed perfect white teeth smiled at him from a partly decomposed human head.

With a croak of horror and disgust Adam jerked his hand back. As he did so the additional weight at his left hand caused the roots to come away, his hands missed the rope and he fell back into the chimney. His heels hit the floor first but his body was leaning backward past the point of vertical recovery. He keeled over. The back of his head struck a dome of rock in the floor with a sodden thud. All the momentum of his weight and the height of his fall went into the blow. The black hair fell straight back from his forehead onto the ground. Creeping fingers of dark red rapidly spread out from amongst it. A piece of dirt from the heather roots dislodged by his climb fell onto his upturned face. The eyes remained open without flinching.

Clever, rich and unenviably dead, Adam Gray had made a mistake, and it had now been compounded according to the inscrutable processes which men call chance.

*

They were back at the house. Myriam had made a cup of tea for herself and Sally, who seemed numb and stiff with the shock of what had happened. Myriam was about to ask if she could check with Alnwick before she set out when the telephone rang.

"Mrs Heathfield's house. Myriam Gray speaking."

"Alnwick Police Station here. Inspector Arne speaking."

"O, I was just about to ring you before I started out."

"I'm afraid we have some news for you. Not very good news I'm afraid. Is someone with you?"

"Er, yes, Mrs Heathfield." Myriam braced herself at the edge of the void.

"I'm afraid we've found your husband. Please don't think you could have helped by being here. We got to him too late."

"Where was he?" It was all she could think to say.

"Inside a hidden cave called Cropsey's Hole up on Debden Moor. We found his hat. That's what brought us to him. He must have slipped while he was out walking yesterday and been unable to get out. We think he rested there for the night and today made an astonishingly heroic attempt to climb out. We think he slipped at the very top and caught his head in falling."

"Is he ... was he ..."

"He must have died instantly. He was a very brave and resourceful man Mrs Gray. I'm so very sorry we couldn't save him."

"When did it happen?"

"We think about 2.30 p.m. We arrived very shortly after. Tragically too late."

"I see. Thank you."

"Mrs Gray –"

"Yes?"

"Don't rush up here tonight. Snow is forecast and there's nothing you can do. Come up tomorrow."

"Yes ... Thank you ... Thank you."

She put down the receiver.

"He's dead too," she said. "At the same time as Tom."

She put her hand out towards Sally who took it and continued to hold it tightly.

*

"That was a tragedy," said the inspector to anyone who would listen as he closed the report he had been writing.

"If only we had been minutes, almost seconds earlier, or if he could have delayed the climb, or if that dreadful corpse hadn't been there to meet him! Poor sod, no wonder he fell!"

"Well, at least we solved one other mystery in the process of the rescue," someone remarked.

"Yes, I suppose so. Have you got the file out? Thank you. Here, Bell, read that, the cutting from the *Advertiser*."

The constable picked up the fading column of newsprint:

Police on Monday mounted a massive search in the lonely Debden Moors, near Rothbury, after a deserted tent, worth nearly £300, had been discovered in the forest.

The tent appeared to have been standing there for some time and the police are trying to establish the ownership of the property.

"At the moment we do not expect anything sinister," said a local police spokesman. "It is just a matter of tracing the person or persons who abandoned this tent, probably three or four months ago."[†]

"Do you think that body was the man, sir?"

"Probably. The state of decomposition fits in with the report on the tent affair. I don't suppose we shall ever know for certain. The body had nothing on it apart from a handkerchief and some coins – a sort of non-person. But he had unusual teeth. According to the pathologist's report there wasn't a single fault or filling in them. Must have been a very healthy chap when he broke his neck in that trivial little crack he was stuck in."

[†] The full text of the report from which the above is quoted may be found on the front page of the *Alnwick Advertiser* for 12 February 1981.

Blaeweary

But I hae dream'd a dreary dream,
Beyond the Isle of Sky;
I saw a dead man win a fight,
And me thought that man was I.
Old Ballad

I normally go straight home at the end of term and stay there. But I had been working all autumn on a new edition of Duns Scotus which incorporated for the first time *De Abysso*, that strange work – I still had doubts whether it was by him or not – which had come to light during the demolition of the old manse at Blackadder, and, truth to tell, I felt desperately in need of a rest and an escape from my thoughts before facing the rigours of our family Christmas. Some country hotel or other place near Duns on the Merse of Berwickshire (which had of course been the birthplace of my philosophical labours) would have the advantage of being quite close to home.

I thumbed through the usual guides. The descriptions of cocktail bars, playrooms, Egon Ronay food, bedroom television and central heating with log fires a special feature were so nauseating that I almost did the sensible thing and stayed at home. But a small announcement in *Country Life* had caught my attention some time earlier, and after much rummaging I found it again.

"Blaeweary County House Hotel," it said. "A warm and comfortable private residence at the skirts of the Lammermuirs. Good plain wholesome food. Well-stocked library. Open all the year. Children not catered for." The description was encouraging; the absence of children decisive. I picked up the phone. After an interminable delay the operator found her way through the thirteen-digit code number to the Oldcastle exchange, and then on to the hotel which was, I recollect, something like Oldcastle 45. Anyway it had more the sound of a good vintage than of a telephone number. The proprietor was helpful and well spoken. Yes he had a room. Only a retired clergyman living there at the moment. I booked for two nights. Would I need to be met at Tillmouth station? No, I would drive. I put the phone down feeling very pleased with the outcome. The Tillmouth branch had of course been closed since the 1947 floods. He had presumably meant to say Berwick.

It was with the utmost sense of freedom and delight in a task completed that I set out in the afternoon a few days later to drive the sixty miles or so round the edge of the Cheviots from my home to Oldcastle. The winter sun hung clear and low in the sky, drawing out long, early shadows from the hills. The trees were sharp against frozen fields, the sky clear.

At Oldcastle I slowed down. It was by then late afternoon and the village looked disappointingly drab and very quiet. It was bigger than I had expected. There was a scattered main street of low cottages, several of which were empty, with a few shops hiding behind red sandstone exteriors of convenanting plainness. Two churches and a bar completed the picture, together with a collection of council houses which must have been entries in a competition to produce the ugliest possible human dwelling. The post office was identified by a black and white notice over a cottage door. I stopped and asked for the hotel.

"Ye'll no be frae these parts?" was the case supposed in answer to my question. The old lady was obviously the clearing house for village news as well as mail.

I agreed, and added helpfully that I was just staying at the hotel for a few days, having seldom been in "these parts" before.

"Ay, just so," she said non-committably. Then after a pause: "It's down the Tillmouth road about two or three mile. Ye'd better take the left fork by the old brig at the end o' the village."

I thanked her and, feeling obliged to make some return for her information, bought half a dozen stamps. She gave them to me without a word. Just as I was going out of the door she called, "Ye'll get a decent night's rest at Mrs Macleucher's across the way."

"I wish I'd known before," I said, thanking her again. "But I'm already booked in at the hotel."

The first tiny cloud on the day had been the dreariness of Oldcastle itself. For some reason I had expected a miniature Jedburgh. The second was the old postmistress's slight reluctance to direct me to Blaeweary. A whisper of unease again settled on my mind when I saw the rather sad gatelodge and curving avenue of overgrown trees leading to the hotel. But the house itself, half a mile up the drive, was well kept. It was one of those immensely robust but slightly overcast and unimaginative imitations of Abbotsford with which every Clydeside laird in the nineteenth century sought to proclaim his substantial membership of an older order of things. Its dark castellated porch stuck out into a half moon of reasonably tidy gravel, and its long mullioned windows disappeared at the corners into absurd little pepperpot towers and areas of complicated slate roof. The gravel forecourt faced directly south, onto bare, frozen pastures. To the rear, big trees opened their spiderwork of branches, black against the winter sky. No one seemed interested in my arrival, and I entered the hall feeling vaguely like an intruder.

On one side were the principal rooms; on the other an enormous staircase sloped discreetly round a stair-well which rose to the full height of the house and finished in an elaborate roof-light of coloured glass. The place was ill lit, but warm and well furnished with large Victorian stuff. In a few minutes a short, plump little woman appeared in response to my pressing a bell marked "reception". She pointed out the dining room, set with a dozen or so tables; the library, a joy to behold with a splendid fire burning; and my bedroom, another large room more or less over the entrance, with its door opening from a wide landing at the top of the stairs. The landing continued as a corridor on either side to other bedrooms. Dinner would be at seven. I began to feel distinctly easier about the situation.

After dressing in comfortable house clothes I went down to the library. No one was there. The collection was more extensive than excellent, but as I wandered round it struck me that much of it was of a piece. One press in particular caught my eye. It was a boy's library. But not of recent period. There were masses of Conan Doyle, Taffrail, Richmal Crompton, early W.E. Johns, and a fair mixture of Sexton Blake, *Rover*, *Wizard* and *Hotspur* annuals. The rest of the library evinced an adult taste of the same period – Walpole, Linklater, Buchan, Wells, Galsworthy and the rest, as well as the usual classics and works of reference. But nothing much seemed to have been added after the end of the war. The latest books were the annuals which stopped at Christmas 1946. It was all light stuff, but suited my mood very well. I picked up one of the Taffrails – *Cypher K* I think it was called – and settled by the fire. "To Peter with love from Father" was written inside the flyleaf.

I read undisturbed for an hour or so. The atmosphere of the house was more like a large, empty, slightly unmanageable private dewelling than an hotel, and I wondered if the proprietor was a member of the original family. My musings were cut short by the arrival of another guest who walked tremulously to the chair opposite me. I noticed leather slippers, tweed stockings drawn over thin legs, clerical collar too large for the shrunken neck, and an old but well-kept suit of brown tweed jacket and knee breeches. He sat down and smiled a little vaguely.

"You will be Mr Littlejohn," he said in a careful, frail, culti-vated voice. "We were expecting you. My name is Martindale. How do you do. Have you met Captain and Mrs Strahan yet?"

I said I had not.

"Yes, they do not usually appear before dinner. The captain is not as young as he was. I see you have found a book. I always read before dinner ... but nothing to disturb one at the time of the flood."

"Er ... no," I said trying vainly to connect ideas of flood and dinner. I sincerely hoped he was not going to continue talking. I have always found the company of familiar books easier than that of unfamiliar people. Moreover, the conversation of the deaf and the very old is demanding and sometimes pointless. But polite-ness seemed to require that I make some sort of contribution.

"Have you stayed here long?" I asked.

"Since I retired. Since I retired. I usually go and stay with my daughter-in-law at the anniversary. But not this year. I ... I ... think she is ill. It is very disturbing you know. I hope you will be happy here. No one really understands ... Perhaps that's all ..."

His head nodded forward softly on to his chest and I thankfully discerned sleep in the aged face. Without otherwise moving I lowered my eyes to my book. Only the occasional turning of a page disturbed the silence until dinner.

I sat alone at my own table with the cleric to my right, and a couple I presumed to be Captain Strahan and his wife tucked away in a corner to my left. They too were old – well into their seventies I would judge – but the captain had a firm, almost hard look about his face which argued anything but dotage, and his wife appeared to be directing the activity of the waitress (the same who had met me earlier) and commenting upon the food in a way which was alert and authoritative. At intervals they conversed quietly. But neither of them ever seemed to laugh or smile. At the end of the meal the captain got up and walked over to my table.

"Good evening," he said. "My name is Strahan." His speech was formal, short; his voice dry and tired. "I hope you will be comfortable while you are staying with us. If there is anything you require you must let me or Jessie know. Apart from the kitchen staff, Jessie is our maid-of-all-work in the winter. But we don't keep anyone on the premises at night, except during the season."

I said something to the effect that I quite understood and would need nothing more after so good a meal, except perhaps a half of one of the rather good clarets I had noticed on the wine list.

"Will you be in to lunch tomorrow?" he asked, looking out of the window behind me.

"I don't think so. I intend to drive over to Duns for a look round, and then maybe take a walk in the afternoon if it's fine, possibly down the old railway if I can find it."

Strahan had been speaking to me with the remote courtesy which was all that the occasion required. But he was giving me only part of his attention, like a man listening for some other sound behind the obvious noises of the room. As I said "railway" he switched all his attention on to me. For a moment I looked into dark, hunted eyes in which I saw anger, or possibly fear. Then the moment had passed.

"Good night," he said briskly. "Breakfast is between eight and ten o'clock."

I made my way to the library, slightly puzzled by the encounter with Strahan. Martindale was nowhere to be seen, and after making up the fire I sat down to what was intended to be a long, quiet read. It was indeed quiet, but the measure was over full. I read for a time: an hour or two I suppose; anyway, long enough to finish the book. One part of me wanted to be alone. To be silent. To be far from any need to respond to the many strangers who flocked through my life. But another part of me was being set on edge by the absolute stillness. After all, I *was* in a hotel. Somebody must be about. I looked into the hallway. A single bulb burned in the murky old chandelier over the stairwell. There was total silence. Surely the proprietor must have some nook of his own where he could watch television or listen to the radio or burst into song with his wife? I walked over to the main door, and looked out across the gravel forecourt. One or two small flakes of snow drifted thoughtfully down. Somewhere far away across the frozen fields a dog howled miserably. A car passed on a road I could not see. The house on either side of the solitary light of the porch was dark. I was tempted to walk round looking for the lights of other occupants, but it was cold and I abandoned the idea, hurrying back to the library. Not long afterwards I made my way up to bed, more or less convinced that I was either alone in the house that evening, or that everyone else slept.

No one could complain about the comfort of the place. A hot-water bottle lay in the bed and, of all things, there was a coal fire in the grate. I was so astounded to see it I half backed out again thinking I was in the wrong room before I caught sight of my own things on the bed. And yet for no consciously justifiable reason I carefully locked the door. But against whom or what I could not say.

The last thing I did before lying down was to look out of the window overlooking the porch. The night was an opaque grey rather than pitch black, and a thin scratching on the glass warned of more snow. I hoped it would not be a heavy fall. The bed was warm and soft. I lay watching the fire send long shadows leaping and dancing across the ceiling, and remembered being a child in the nursery at home when one of us was ill. There was peace, and I sunk quickly into those moments of relaxation which just precede sleep. The dog was still howling somewhere beyond the abyss of night. The sound wove its way in and out of my sleep. I would be with friends in a summer garden, or punting down slow streams of autumn long ago, when I would hear it again at the edge of my dream, and I would half waken in an empty land.

The next morning passed quickly and pleasantly. I had a good breakfast – alone, but the others had obviously been there before me. Jessie was pottering about.

"You come in early?" I said.

"Oh yes sir. I just live a wee bit down the road."

"I wouldn't care to walk all that way down the drive in the pitch dark." The remark sounded foolish.

"Oh it's nothing when you know every step, and I wouldn't want to stay ..."

She seemed on the point of continuing her sentence but instead made it a full stop, and busied herself with the cutlery. There was an enigmatic reticence about the occupants of Blaeweary which positively provoked curiosity! I was about to ask her more about the place when she departed on a call from the kitchen.

The snow had not been heavy enough to prevent motoring. I spent the morning at Duns, and had a lunch of bread and cheese and a half of beer in the Black Bull. Then I drove slowly back to Oldcastle and on to Blaeweary, changed into rougher outdoor clothes and boots, and walked out across the frosty fields in front of the house. A mile or so to the south I found the old railway. My bedroom window must have looked directly across to it, but nothing had been visible from the house since the track lay in a long cutting which curved gently away, deep and shadowy, in both directions from the point where I stood.

I scrambled down the overgrown bank. The snow was slightly thicker where the rails had been, and lay in an unbroken white strip. Everything was cold and still. The low altitude of the winter sun could not have reached the floor of the cutting at mid-day, and one side was now in deep shadow. I started walking briskly. About half a mile on, the track straightened out and a high single arch bridge came into view, black against the snow. As I walked towards it I looked up, partly expecting to see a face peering over the stone parapet, as small boys are wont to look down from railway bridges. But of course the trains that passed had long since puffed away into the memories of children who were now busy with the cares of other generations, and no one looked at me. A hundred yards farther on I came to a halt. The cutting ended abruptly at a small river and continued as an embankment on the far side. But the bridge had been removed, or washed away, and the banks were steep and icy. It was quite impossible to go on, and

I retraced my steps. I had just reached the bridge again, and was looking up at it when the stillness was broken by a single rustling sigh of air which shook snow from the withered bracken and set the dry grasses scratching and tinkling against each other. Almost at the same time a sound came back at me from the arch of the bridge. It was, I think, the wind whistling for a few moments in some fault in the stonework. It had the quality of an echo, audible but somehow unreal; distinct and yet not quite from where it seemed to originate. Forlorn and desolate in the winter cold, it caused me to shiver. I climbed up the embankment to the bridge expecting to find some explanation for the sound, but there was nothing. Only hoar-frost on the untouched grass, a quiet sunset, and no moving thing in the landscape.

The bridge itself was little more than a stone cattle creep between two fields. Below me the railway was again silent. I could see the lie of the land at once: the cutting bending away to the east, to the west the track straightening out, and then interrupted at the missing bridge, to the north the house. It was closer than I expected, and loomed up out of the fields – a dark, two-dimensional cut-out with large red windows flashing back the last horizontal rays of the sun. I was half way back to it, and walking quickly, when I heard the sound again, as it seemed to me, an eerie, remote, fearful cry of woe drawn into the silence of a universe which comprehended nothing of such things.

Everything else remained as silent as a painting. I hurried on. Before I reached the house the sun had set below the distant Cheviots, and the windows of Blaeweary turned a pale luminous pink which suddenly darkened to black as I reached the gravel of the forecourt.

I will not say I was frightened, but all the ease and pleasure of the day had gone. Part of me said it was a lost dog. Part of me said it was a breath of wind sounding in something on the old railway. But part of me said it was not the wind, and not an animal lost, but an animal calling, and at the back of my mind hovered the unnerving feeling that it was calling *me*.

I did not expect anyone to sympathize, but I did at least want to talk to someone. As usual no one was to be found, not even the old clergyman in the library, and I hesitated to dig Jessie or the cook out of the kitchen for what would certainly seem to them a matter of no concern. In the end I simply adopted that universal opiate for the troubled soul: I changed, had a hot bath, ordered a glass of whisky and went down to the library.

Martindale was already asleep in his chair by the fire, a little wizened stick of a man somehow housed in those ancient tweeds. He did not waken when Jessie brought in my drink. I picked up a book and sat down feeling much more at peace with things. In a few minutes the old man twitched. I looked up to discover him gazing at me.

"You must be Mr Littlejohn," he said without moving.

"Yes I am. We met last night."

"That is very interesting. We don't often have visitors at this season you know. The local people never come here in December. Not since the terrible flood. Silly rumours you know."

"What flood was that?" I asked recollecting something he had mentioned the previous evening.

"Flood? Is there one?" He looked round as if to see if it might be in the house.

"No, the flood you mentioned."

"I don't think so. Not since the railway closed. You must come back in February if you want to see one."

I tried another line of approach. "Has Captain Strahan lived here long?"

"Nowhere else. He was a boy here. But he's very old now. He has been since the death of his son ... I sometimes fear for him ... But you must excuse me, I have to finish this book before dinner and ... it may slip away ... before I have mastered it."

His head – the head of an old turtle perched precariously on a turkey's neck – sunk forward on his chest and he apparently fell asleep again. I had noticed some of the discordant oddities at Blaeweary, and Martindale seemed to have solved some puzzles for me. Strahan's son must have been killed somehow in the disastrous floods of 1947, the year the book collection stopped. The thought was disturbing, and I tried to put it out of my mind.

I had dinner alone. Martindale's was brought into the library on a tray by Jessie when she came to tell me mine was ready. The dinner was good, very good – Palestine soup, poached turbot, and mutton chops which I washed down with a very tolerable half-bottle of Ch. Montrose. I was returning to the library when Jessie caught up with me.

"His reverence bid me say to you he was sorry if he was rude to you about not wanting to talk. Only he's more used to books than people, and finds conversation with young folks very difficult. That's what he said sir. Will you be wanting anything before I go?" she added in the same breath.

"I don't think so, thank you. But tell me, am I alone in the house at night? I mean are Captain and Mrs Strahan on the premises?"

"Oh yes, but they keep rooms at the back of the house. On the quiet side you know."

Her words gave me a convenient opening. "There is one thing," I said, "I meant to speak about it to Captain Strahan if I'd seen him at dinner. I heard a lost dog last night and again down on the railway today. I wonder ... ." Then, as I hesitated: "There's no lost dog," she said firmly and in a low voice.

"But Jessie, I heard it."

For the second time that day I felt myself on the verge of receiving an explanation – almost a confidence – but again Jessie retreated from it.

"Never mind what ye heard. There's no lost dog, and there's nae thing to hurt or be hurt if we a' keep our ain peace. Now if ye'll excuse me I must get home."

The statement admitted no refusal, and I returned unsatisfied to the now empty library, Martindale having retreated to whatever inconspicuous corner of the mansion he occupied.

With the banging of the front door, as Jessie or the cook left some time later, the same sense of desertion and emptiness settled upon the house I had experienced the previous night. But it was not the same. On the first night the house had been dead and empty. Now it was alive, waiting, expectant. A light wind made doors creak. Bushes rustled and tapped at the windows, and it was colder, much colder. With something of this in mind I went up to my bedroom to check the fire. It had been lit, and I banked it up from the hod of coal. I had my hand on the library door again when I heard it, a moan of desolate loneliness from somewhere outside the house, but nearer and more insistent. I entered the library and quickly closed the door.

Now that I am trying to write this down so that the telling of it might bring some peace, I wish that someone else had been with me – not as then, for the support of human company, but because I need to know if another person would have had the experiences I had. It wasn't imagination. By all that's real, I know the difference between what I see, and what is vague, or uncertain, or of doubtful veracity. I am a critical man. I know myself. I am the same sceptic now that I was then. And somehow I brought that to my aid even at the time. Let me try to be clearer.

I sat for a while in the library listening to the ordinary sounds of the night. The wind rattled the great sash windows. A loose slate, or something else up on the roof, was tapping and banging. The coals in the fireplace were sucking and pulling lustily as a good fire should. But behind it all, outside, the other sound was there. I strained all my faculties to discern what manner of thing it was, and whether it receded or approached. Sometimes it seemed the one, sometimes the other. But I was like the stranded swimmer watching the tide, and I knew it came inexorably closer. However, the very act of concentrating upon the disturbance, thinking about it, enquiring into its nature in isolation from the purely circumstantial bumps and creaks of the night, and analyzing its possible causes, began to disarm the thing. After all, I was perfectly safe physically. A dog or weird animal outside could not get in – or so I assured myself; and if it did, what of it? The creature, if it was a creature, was in distress, lost or hurt, not malevolent. So I ought to go out and see if I could help. But there I stuck. It had to be some freak of the wind, whatever the aura of purpose and movement it seemed to possess.

I took up some book or other – I forget its title, but it worked like ear-phones on an aircraft. For a time I was in another world, listening to another voice. But the reading had to end. At about eleven o'clock I stood up to go to bed. Outside, a cold draft of air swept across the hall and up the stairs. As I climbed to my room the thought entered my head that a door or window was open somewhere at the front of the house. Involuntarily I hurried. I had forgotten that in my usual over-prudent way I had locked the bedroom door. The key was in my pocket, and caught in the lining as I tried to get it out. The delay enhanced the unpleasant feeling that something was behind me on the stairs, and once inside I shut the door and locked it hastily before pausing to listen. But there were no sounds of pursuit. I ought to have been satisfied. Instead, guided by a glow from the fire, I made my way across to the window and cautiously divided the curtains with finger and thumb.

I had anticipated a totally dark night. An almost full moon shone brilliantly over fields that looked as if they had been sprinkled with salt to produced everywhere a grey glitter. Indeed it was brighter outside than in. I could see clearly the fields and patches of black trees between the house and where I had walked on the hidden railway. Then I looked down at the gravel forecourt, in time to see, but not to see properly, a movement at the edge of the moonlit area as something disappeared into the shadow of the porch immediately below. It did not re-appear. In my own mind I was now certain that an entrance had been opened for whatever it was to come into the house, and with all my being I did not want it to get in. I suppose I thought to guard the door. Anyway, I moved across in time to hear a creak on the staircase and then, after an interval of silence, a sort of slow sweeping sound, a dragging, scratching; like an animal pulling something wet behind it. I tell myself I ought to have looked out. But I could not. Something repulsive, something truly from the pit, was, I believed, at the other side of my door, and no reasoning known to man could have induced me to open it at that moment. But the thing passed, dragging along the polished oak floor to my right. I waited, maybe seconds, maybe minutes. I've no idea. It had gone. I *felt* its absence. But I still waited. Nothing. Eventually curiosity, and perhaps the need to see that it had gone, overcame imagined horrors. I quietly unlocked the door and edged it open. The absurd single bulb burned steadily and boldly in the great chandelier over the stairwell. There was nothing to see. Whatever had been at my door had gone. But surely it would have left some mark from the outside world? I bent down and brushed my hand over the polished wood. Nothing at all. With a last scrutiny of the corridor to the left and right, I backed into my room, puzzled and disconcerted.

Now at this stage I ought to have gone to bed. In fact I sat miserably by the fire filling my imagination with all sorts of things that thinking should have kept under control. I was brought back to reality – yes I use the word advisedly – by the unmistakable sound of a door banging somewhere at the rear of the house, and then what I took to be footsteps on the gravel. I glanced at my watch. It was almost a quarter to one. For the second time that night I peeped out.

I saw what I was half expecting to see – Strahan walking slowly round the side of the house and across the forecourt leaving bold black footprints as he went. I heard his feet in the gravel, and I saw his footmarks dark in the thin covering of now-thawing snow. I also saw a large black shadow which passed over the snow behind him and left no mark at all. Strahan looked back once, but it was at the house, not at what followed him, and it seemed to me, as I watched him walk away across the fields, that he had not seen his companion. I turned away as he disappeared from sight and lay down shivering on the bed. At some time he returned, for I heard his footsteps, but I was too timid to stir from my bed to find out if he was alone. For most of the night I remained awake listening.

In the morning I rose early and went down to breakfast. Strahan was there, so was Martindale, but Strahan's wife was absent. I walked over to the proprietor's table having worked myself up into something like anger over my disrupted night.

"I would be grateful for a few words with you before I depart."

"If you wish Mr Littlejohn. I trust nothing is wrong."

I looked at him and said, "I was plagued rather badly yesterday by the howling of a lost dog and in the early part of the night it came into the house. I wonder if you could shed any light on the matter?"

As I spoke he went so pale I almost relented my boldness, but he rallied and said quickly: "I shall be pleased to speak with you. May we leave it until after breakfast. Jessie will take you to my study."

When we had all finished eating, Jessie came over to my table and said Captain Strahan would see me now. The expression was curious, implying somehow that I was the supplicant, but I followed Jessie down some steps, across the kitchen, up more steps, along a corridor and into a room of modest size comfortably furnished as an office and study. Captain Strahan was sitting at the desk facing me. He rose as I entered.

"Please sit down," he said. "You say you heard a dog yesterday. I wonder if I could ask you to describe what you heard. Please forgive me. I am not doubting your word but the matter is of great importance to me, and I would like to be clear about it." He spoke with a sincerity which gave me no wish to dispute with him.

I told him exactly what I had seen and heard, beginning at the railway and concluding with my observing him walk away across the fields. But I did not say I had actually seen the dog, nor did I describe its macabre condition, nor the circumstance I dared not mention. He listened with rapt attention and when I had finished I thought I could detect an expression almost akin to relief in his face.

"Mr Littlejohn," he began slowly, "you are, unless my judgment errs unusually, a man of discernment and I shall tell you a story which I would not wish the ears of fools to hear. I shall tell you, because in some way I do not understand you have become a partner in an experience which has been mine alone for more than thirty years. You saw the books in the library?" I nodded. "Most were my son's. You saw the missing bridge over the Backwater on the railway just beyond the cutting?" Again I nodded. "The cause of my son's death. I was busy, and young, and just back from the war, and we had opened this place as a hotel. It was austerity you know, and we grew most of our own food. My boy was twelve, and a fine lad. He would often go out for walks by himself with his dog Kitchener, and never took any harm. I seldom had time to go with him. One evening in December – yesterday was the anniversary – it was a night of a brilliant full moon and Peter asked me to come for a walk with him."

He suddenly lowered his voice and looked down at the table. "I was too busy," he said. "His mother was ill with flu, and I didn't hear him go out. There was a tremendous flood of waters going down the river from a temporary thaw in the Lammermuirs. He must have walked down to the railway, and along it, and seen the bridge had gone. We think he ran back down the line to stop the last train from Tillmouth. He knew all the train times by heart and used to watch them from the little stone bridge. But in the moonlight, and with the curve of the railway, the driver didn't see him in time. The engine must have hit Kitchener as well, but didn't kill him. He came up here for me. I heard him howling in the distance, but I didn't understand. At least, I don't think I did. I was busy. He found me in an upstairs room, down the corridor from yours. He died there. Of course then I knew something was desperately wrong. I looked out of the window, saw the plume of steam from the stranded train in the moonlight; the driver had brought it to a halt just short of the missing bridge. It was the last train that ever came from Tillmouth. The rest you may guess."

I was looking down at the floor when he finished speaking, a tight constraint in my throat. I understood. I understood more than I could say.

"Every year, Mr Littlejohn, every December on the day of the flood, I, and until now I alone, hear Peter's dog begging me to go down to help my son, and every year I go, and there is peace for a while."

I found my voice. "You mean *no one* has ever heard it apart from you?"

"No one until you yourself. At first I asked the servants, but they just thought I was becoming deranged or fey, and their talk gave the place an odd reputation down in the village. Old Martindale half believes me, but can offer no help. Not even my wife hears it, although she does believe that it's not just an old record of regret playing itself in my head."

"You have never seen the dog sir?" The address of respect came quite unbidden to me, but it was the just acknowledgment of the man's burden and the dignity with which he carried it.

"Never. There is nothing to see."

"If I said to you that Kitchener's injuries were all to his hindquarters, and that he was a large black Labrador, would you still say there was nothing to see?"

He rose slowly from his chair looking at me. "I didn't tell you about Kitchener did I?"

"No you didn't tell me. May we leave it at that?"

"As you wish," he said, but I could not read the expression on his face.

We remained silent, and then he said rather suddenly, "I suppose it's too much to expect you to come here again?"

I said I'd be happy to recommend Blaeweary to anyone who asked me.

"It is no matter. We are near the end of our road here, and then the long silence or perhaps ... perhaps ..." His eyes had a distant look of wistful hope for a moment. Then coming back to himself he added, "There will of course be no charge for your room."

I held my hand to him. "Goodbye," I said.

We shook hands, total strangers really, but with a bond of shared experience too deep for words. The last thing he said was, "I've waited half a lifetime for someone who would understand. It lightens the load you know."

I left him sitting there alone, an old, frail, upright man, dignified by long grief which he would never lighten by self-forgiveness.

I drove slowly home, depressed and sad, in the wet thaw that had begun in the night. On the way I stopped at our family church to put a few winter flowers on the grave of that other little boy whose father had also been too engrossed in his work to go with him when he was lost in the flooded Hearthope Burn. I understood. I understood too well. I should have told him when I had the chance. Now I can only tell you who will never know me.

Single to Burnfoot

Gods of my hearth let me return.
You know me when I come alone:
A traveller weary from the road,
A wayfarer returning home.

You know me like a welcome friend:
Though I am young and you are old,
And still your presence by the hearth
Keeps nightly watch against the cold.

I know not fear, familiar gods.
The beam that creaks, the coals that fall,
The rose bush tapping at the glass,
The shadows dancing on the wall,

I know you as familiar things.
You warm my soul and give me rest.
We smile together, though I come
A mortal and a passing guest.

But, kindest gods, you too must die
And perish in the length of years.
We both are mortals, you and I,
Though only I have mortal fears.

Gods of my hearth let me return.
I pass the threshold of the door,
I walk again the road of life,
I leave you waiting as before.

Tossan

James Wynchcombe placed the spectacles carefully upon his nose and peered short-sightedly down the platform. There was no sign of the train which would carry him away from the revamped iron Gothic which had been for so many years the gateway to his work, and the hallmark of stability. He paced up and down several times, inspected the labels on his luggage, bought a paper and pretended to read it, tucked it under his arm and looked for the train again. Nothing indicated it was any nearer. He looked at his watch and checked it fussily and ostentatiously with the platform clock. The impression conveyed to anyone watching was of a man who had an important business appointment, and who was fretting about the train being late. But the train was not late, and James had no appointment, and anyway no one was watching. He was simply exhausted, and at the beginning of an enforced holiday. But fuss and hurry had become so much his habit of life that he carried the manner of responding to genuine problems and delays into everything he did, whether he was exhausted or not, which was why his doctor had suggested a couple of weeks away from work, people and noise. The obvious place was his youthful haunt around Burnfoot in the north, a district which had not yet suffered the invasion of dual carriageways and development corporations, caravans and leisure areas. He had even heard that tourists were comparatively rare. Yes, that was where he would go; and crushing the last hesitations about returning to a place where he had been so happy so long ago, he found himself looking over the line to the platform where he usually waited for the city train.

His reveries were interrupted by the roar of a powerful engine as the express entered the station. He glanced at his watch and noted, with approval, that "The North Briton" came most carefully upon its hour. There was for once nothing to worry about. He had reserved a seat – first class, non-smoker, in the corner, window side facing the engine (he had always been of that race of forward-looking men who liked to see where they were going rather than where they have been). He had even secured the services of a porter, a species generally held to be extinct. How pleasant it was to stand aside from the rush for the best seats – those moments of possessive individualism which no socialist theory could ever erode – and how easy to stand aside when one already has the best seat!

James curled up comfortably in his corner and resolved that he was going to enjoy the express journey before he was handed over to the vicissitudes of the bus company which he had been told would take him the last ten miles to Burnfoot, and the hospitality of the Bertram Arms. The only other occupants of the compartment were a large gentleman in a suit of formal cut, who was sleeping in a very decisive manner, and a thin angular woman of indefinite age and unusual height who held up a copy of *Woman's Journal* as if it were a first-strike weapon in the war of the sexes. She looked out of the window only on the side away from the other occupants of the carriage and with an air of offended disapproval. No interrogation was to be feared from those quarters.

The train moved out of the station with a steady, swift acceleration which was very pleasant, and he was looking down at suburban scenes of prosperity and industry. It was not an attractive prospect he realized, though he had so long accepted it as part of the structure of his life that he failed to see its ugliness most of the time. Within a few miles it gave way to an uneasy co-existence of industry and agriculture. A rather sad, down-trodden little river wound about beneath the railway embankment, and a wide modern highway kept them company, punctuated by newly planted dead trees, and petrol stations apparently intent upon giving away more value than they sold. The fields looked sour and badly drained, and the industry which broke up the arable land seemed to be mostly disused quarries, with the inevitable accompaniment of weed-grown slag heaps and ruined brick cottages. He turned away and fell asleep. It was better not to see some things, and sleep was all he really wanted.

He woke with a jerk at the call of "second lunches please", and got up hastily and in momentary confusion to follow the restaurant-car attendant, for he still took an almost schoolboyish delight in feeding on a train. Seated in the restaurant car he noted a change in the countryside: in the west high and distant hills began to appear, while in the east a certain nearness of the horizon suggested a falling of the land down to the sea.

"Where have we got to?" he asked the waiter who brought the soup.

"Just past Newsteads, sir," answered the man, lurching away on his other errands just as the train negotiated an unexpectedly sharp bend.

James was surprised at the length of time he had slept, and it was not long after he had finished eating that he began to consider the problem of disembarkation.

He was unclear why the main-line express stopped at Wintonhope. It was only afterwards he was told it did so only on Fridays in summer, by request, and that they didn't really like doing it. However, on that particular day the train did stop, and he found himself out on the platform with the guard bundling his cases after him with remarkable alacrity. In a few seconds the express was a diminishing speck and its roar had diffused into silence.

His own side appeared to contain the few administrative offices, and across the line was only a single platform with a chair proclaiming the name of the station. Nowhere was there any sign of a bus, or a taxi, or a car, or a road. The absolute silence was a little disturbing after the companionable bustle of the express, and he turned to inspect the noticeboards which ought to tell him how long he would have to wait for the connecting bus or local diesel car. They informed him that there would be a fête in Brinkburn Priory on Saturday, July the first, and that a special excursion train would run at 2 p.m. that day. This was very interesting, only he had it in mind that the first of July had been a Wednesday that year. He regarded the notice with disfavour, and was about to turn away when the heading of the board, in faded yellow letters too fat for their height, caught his eye:

WINTONHOPE AND BURNFOOT RAILWAY CO.

What an extraordinary survival! It would be worth securing for a railway museum. But this was hardly an apt moment to start collecting railway installations as souvenirs.

James walked down the platform and tried to whistle, but nothing came, and his leather heels on the flagstones echoed noisily. He had turned about several times, debating what to do next, when he found that it was difficult to remember clearly which direction the train had taken leaving the station. Both ways looked the same, and some confusion made him feel it had departed the way it had come in. The whole situation was becoming most distressing. Surely he couldn't have been misinformed about the bus? Someone must be found! He cleaned his spectacles carefully, and then turned his attention to the door marked "Staff Only", knocking with a greater show of authority and confidence than he felt. Nothing happened, and the rather hollow sound suggested, he had to admit, not only the absence of people, but the absence of furniture as well. He knocked again, less convincingly, and with no more result.

He had become so accustomed to planning well in advance the last detail of his life that he felt, as he gazed in mute dismay at the brown weatherworn door, as though the very gates of civilization and order had been slammed in his face (for no very good reason) by an inconsiderate and inconsequential providence. Several equally unattractive alternatives were beginning to flit about the back of his mind. Perhaps he would have to walk (horror!) the ten, or was it fifteen miles to Burnfoot? Fifteen he felt sure, but which way lay the road? And he saw with rising alarm what he had at first only half noticed: that no track left the station in any direction over the green waterlogged undulations that lay all round. There was no possibility of a bus. But what had that fool in the enquiry office told him ... ? Had he been put off at the wrong station by some evil chance? Perhaps he would have to camp down in the station waiting-room for the night! But the thought appalled him and brought visions of cold, and rats, and rheumatism. Then again a train might come, but for some reason, though he had only been waiting ten minutes – no it must be more than that, to add to his confusion his watch had stopped – he had ceased to believe in a train or a bus to Burnfoot. In the chilly twilight of an early October afternoon the place didn't look as though it had seen transport for fifty years ... the aptness of the thought forced itself alarmingly into the front of his mind. Yes, that was exactly what the station looked like; the only signs of late twentieth century industry were the glittering steel rails which swept between the platforms. He looked out to where the railway curved out of sight into a cutting on the moor. Beyond the cutting, mist lay across the empty landscape in white folds. Very slowly he allowed his eyes to follow the curve of the track back towards the station, and to linger in surprise and incomprehension on the grass growing between the sleepers ... and the rust ... He suddenly felt desperately lonely and rather ill. The mist closed in like a blanket.

"Will you be looking for a train to Burnfoot ?" The voice at his side startled him like the sudden waking from a bad dream.

"Of course I am! What the hell else would I be doing in this godforsaken place? Where is it!"

"Not far away," replied the station master, answering his question literally. "But perhaps you are cold, and would like to come into my office and warm yourself while you are waiting?"

"Thank you." He repressed a question about how long the train would be, and followed the man uncertainly towards the "Staff Only" door.

His companion was short, not much over five foot five, and supported a curiously large moustache, divided in the middle and drooping down either side of his mouth. The rest of his head was almost enveloped in a large black regulation cap, and he spoke slowly and deliberately, with the suspicion of a west of Scotland lilt. This much he observed by the time they entered the office.

It was more inviting than he had anticipated: delightfully warm and cosy in an old-fashioned, cluttered-up way; with plenty of brown varnish, group photographs, well-worn black leather chairs, and a desk heaped up with all manner of official bric-à-brac – stamps, rulers, cups, pipes, pens and large half-empty bottles of ink. The details were very clear.

"Will you take a cup of tea?" asked his host.

"Thank you, it would be much appreciated," he said, recovering his good temper. "You must forgive my rudeness outside, only I'd been looking for someone and you startled me." He apologized to his own surprise. It was a long time since he had apologized to anyone for what might reasonably be called their own fault, and it made him feel remarkably good. He must do more of it.

"It's a very quiet, old-fashioned station you have here. You don't get much traffic through I imagine," he ventured.

"Not much now, not many want to come this way, but there's always a service for such as need it."

"That's rather unusual, I thought they'd cut out all that sort of thing?"

The old man looked up from the black, battered stove where he was pouring out tea, and for the first time James saw his eyes.

They were hazel grey, and full of peace and gentleness.

"Do you then value everything by the number of people who use it? Is there nothing in this world worthwhile for its own sake?"

Somewhat taken aback, he could find nothing to say.

"And why are you going to Burnfoot?" persisted the old man as he handed him a cup of steaming tea.

"I suppose because my doctor told me to. Thank you, I don't take sugar."

"And when, sir, did you last take your doctor's advice, especially when you have always believed that it is a mistake to retrace old steps?"

James considered. He had indeed been half afraid of his doctor's advice to pause in his career and turn away from his work. Years earlier he had not wanted the life he now lived. But need at first, and then responsibility, and finally a wintry stoicism had bound him to the Ixion's wheel of his own endeavour. Now he had woken up in the morning, asking himself what he had achieved that was worth while, what he had given to life. Nothing, came the answer, nothing. And he wanted to go back and to remember, to pick up where he had left off, if it was not already too late. He wanted to be still, and to be at peace. He did not want, and did not need, to go on fighting for the good of other people's money as a successful accountant.

"Then you really want to go back?" said the old man.

"Yes," he said, uncertain whether he had been daydreaming or speaking aloud. "When does the train come?"

"Very soon. Perhaps you will excuse the delay, but there will be no hurry now?"

"Yes, I suppose you are right." He was thinking in ways which had been strange to him for many years. There was a pause. Where was he? What was he doing? Where was he going? he asked himself. Somehow the answers: "nowhere", "nothing" and "home" seemed to present themselves.

"The Burnfoot is here when you are ready," said the old man at length. James put his cup down.

"Thank you, I didn't hear it arrive."

"Perhaps you were dreaming of other things."

They walked out on to the platform, and James indistinctly saw an oddly antique coach pulled by a tank engine running backwards. He couldn't see it clearly, for the mist had drawn in from the moor while they were talking, but he could hear it wheezing and coughing, and could dimly discern its black shape.

He climbed into the compartment and almost at once the train rattled out of the station. He looked across at the sepia photographs of Cragside and Seahouses, and at the antique cut-glass mirror in the centre, suspended above the faded blue upholstery which had once displayed a generous pattern of goblets and grapes. The steam heating hissed, and the carriage rocked and rattled over the rails. Outside the mist seemed to have cleared, and landmarks came into view, familiar to him long ago: the oddly terraced hill that shielded Burnfoot, the little road that wound over and under the railway, the heather slopes and sheep and the last deep wooded gorge, where road and rail and river squeezed through precariously together. This was nearly home.

He lay back in the cushions dreaming happily. The years were falling away from him, and a great weight seemed to be lifting from his back. Here at least things did not change. When he glanced out again he saw to his disappointment that the mist had closed in once more, but in a few minutes the train glided to a halt.

It was very quiet, and he got out deeply preoccupied with his own thoughts and was some way down the street before he realized that he didn't remember handing in his ticket. Still, tomorrow would do if he had, in fact, forgotten.

His hosts at the Bertram Arms welcomed him as he hoped they would – genially and politely, but without thrusting their company upon him. After dinner he chanced to remark to the landlord that the railway seemed a bit out of date, but it worked well. Mr. Parkinson hastened to agree with him, but added "only as far as Wintonhope".

"No, I mean the last part from Wintonhope to here."

"I'm afraid sir, you're making a mistake, trains haven't run here since 1952, and they can't now, there are no rails any longer. There's a good bus service to Wintonhope," he added on the way out. "It runs along the old railway track since there were no roads to Wintonhope station."

James went to bed early that night, tired, but in a very thoughtful mood. He was not sure what had happened to him. One thing he knew – that he was tired in the way that makes for deep sleep. He lay down and drew the white sheets up round him, resolving as he did so that lunatic landlords who didn't even know the transport to their own village could still be congratulated on the comfort of their establishments. But the thought "lunatic landlord" did not completely satisfy him, and he went to sleep more puzzled than he would admit.

The morning broke clear and fresh, full of autumnal smells of damp leaves and mist blowing in from the water meadows. James felt a young man again apart from the slight headache he always got after sleeping too long when he was over-tired. As he shaved, he thought that his hair was even a little less thin on top than it had been the previous morning. His first determination, stronger than the call of breakfast, was to look at the railway station.

It was as his host had said. Cutting and embankment remained, but all was overgrown with weeds and bushes except for a narrow macadamed strip in the centre of the old trackbed. There were no traces of station or rails. He stared at it long and hard, taking off and putting on his spectacles several times as he did so. He had never had a psychical experience of any kind in his life, and didn't believe in them. In any case what had happened was singularly urbane and unalarming, and only he had changed. He had somehow broken out of the wheel of fortune that had borne him on and up so long. He had come home. He was at peace. What matter if he had been so stupid or so sleepy or so short-sighted as to mistake a bus for a railway carriage? And yet it was very strange ...

He looked again at the place where the platform had been, and noticed a small card in the thin grass. It was covered with dew. He picked it up and examined it. In his hand lay an old ticket to Wintonhope, with an extension "service permitting" to Burnfoot. It is now carefully framed, and may be seen above the fireplace of the cottage which he bought in the village. The reverse side is occasionally shown to close friends. On it is printed, "Not transferable; no return journey available". But James Wynchcombe will give no other account of it.

The Dark Companion

"I warn you, my Lord, against this indulgency of evil feeling," said I. "I know not to which it is more perilous, the soul or the reason; but you go the way to murder both."

The Master of Ballantrae

On the north-east corner of the chapel was a small and long-disused graveyard. It was tucked in below the dark granite walls of the sanctuary and fenced off from the kitchen of the college by an iron paling. Those whom their times saw fit to remember lay there in peace, in mute oblivion to the passing of the centuries; their inconspicuous virtues magnified by text and effigy; their vices unrecorded and forgotten. And so perhaps they would have remained, in damp obscurity until the great day of the general resurrection, but for the unforseeable zeal of Henry Flynn: one whose mission as Bursar was to make the crooked straight and the rough places plain.

He had often walked past the little burial ground, but that day, as he later told me, he was particularly looking for underutilized space in college. There is no doubt that the dank little triangle of land was neglected and decayed. The recumbent figures on the tombs were crumbling into ruinous parodies of the human form, and many of the inscriptions were so blackened or eroded that those commemorated could only be identified by recourse to one of the older college histories. Indeed the whole area would probably have been cleared out years ago but for the persistent and unexamined belief among the body corporate that something, somewhere, said that it had to be left as it was in perpetuity – a belief for which Flynn could see no evidence in the computerized records he had himself caused to be generated. He concluded that part of the yard could easily accommodate forty or fifty bicycles, and the remainder could be cleaned up and neatly cobbled to provide a way through to the new laundrette. The bits and pieces of the memorials could be stowed decently away in the boiler house under the chapel – the crypt as it had been.

The thing was done remarkably quickly: approved by a fellows' meeting under a general heading of space ultization. I think it was referred to in the minutes as "*restoration* of disused graveyard". The stone figures were carried away, the ground levelled, and the old gravestones set round the perimeter like dead teeth. Our new Master, the knighted head of a former polytechnic (he was only with us for a short time), took the opportunity to try to decree that there should be no further interments in college. Apparently the modern world demands laundrettes not resting places. Be that as it may, the business did not endear the Bursar to every member of the college, particularly not to me, and it was altogether typical of him.

As a character Flynn was an uncomfortable sort of a man: withdrawn and hostile at times; at other times charming, brutally forthright, erudite or cold in erratic compound. He had come to us out of the civil service after beginning life as some kind of economist, and he still gave occasional lectures. His main idea was to "bring the college into the twentieth century" (or he may have said the twenty-first). As a consequence he was always busy. The graveyard clearance was just an irritating trifle, or so I thought. Earlier, in deference to the idol of the market-place which holds that return on assets must be maximized, he had persuaded (with ease) the Master to allow a permanent exhibition (with entry fee) in the Old Library, and he had bullied the Fellows into opening undergraduate rooms in the summer as bed and breakfast establishments for tourists. It is already evident that the cost of the Residence Officer and the staff who had to be appointed to run these enterprises nullified the advantages the college was supposed to reap from the erosion of its fabric and main purposes. But I digress. I was speaking about Flynn the man.

He was about forty-five, of vigorous physique and considerable stature – easily six foot I would say. I mention this to indicate to whoever may read what follows that the Bursar was neither old, nor fragile, nor, in my considered opinion, in any way unstable. But he was unpredictable with people. He had a great ability to be generous and friendly, but also, when the mood was on him, to be rude to a degree which was exceedingly hurtful. This was the mood in which I met him earlier that evening when I first learnt about his illness. He approached me in the quadrangle and apparently looked straight at me, or over my head, and then walked past without any acknowledgment of my attempt to say good evening to him. It was later the same night that he called unexpectedly at my rooms. I had the fire on, for an east wind was moaning out of the fens which not even I could endure, accustomed as I was to the primaeval chill of one of the oldest sets in college.

THE DARK COMPANION

I welcomed him with rather thin enthusiasm. I had intended to work late and did not want visitors, but as he seemed both uncharacteristically nervous and heavily preoccupied by something I thought it was best to let him have his say. One never knows when a little present interest may secure a future return of capital. As I gave him a sherry I noticed that his hand was unsteady.

After the usual pleasantries and minor analyses of the weather I asked of what use I could be to him.

"I'm afraid I want your help," he said briskly and then, with more hesitation, "I want to talk to someone. I know we don't get on particularly, and I know you don't like the modern view of college I stand for, but I also know you'll keep your own counsel."

I made a noise which could have been taken as assent to either or both of his concluding sentiments. Flynn was always candid. It was one of his more tiresome virtues.

"You know I'm not given to imaginative fancies," he continued with artless understatement, "but things that have happened recently have puzzled me. No, that's not true. I mean I'm worried about something, and I thought you wouldn't mind if I talked to you."

He stopped awkwardly.

"Would you like some more sherry?" I asked. "I have some of the sweet stuff somewhere if you prefer it."

No thanks. You understand I'm not seeking a free consultation out of hours." (I had heard that before from others!) "I just want to talk to someone, and since we both live in college ..."

"Go on, I'm listening."

"Hear me out then. Don't jump to a conclusion at the start. It's not just an hallucination."

"I am not in the habit of jumping to conclusions, Flynn. As I believe you know, before I turned to medicine I read philosophy when that meant careful analysis, linguistic precision and proportioning conclusions to evidence. I am perfectly willing to listen to anything you have to say, and listen in confidence, but please do not preface your remarks by telling me *how* I should listen to you."

"Sorry! I didn't mean to give offence."

I was so surprised at his apology that I was reduced to muttering about all of us needing to talk to someone if there is a problem, a facile little generalization false in my own case; although I suppose the writing of this account is in itself some sort of evidence to the contrary. "You were saying it's not a hallucination," I continued. "So you have been seeing something you can't account for, or which others can't see."

"Yes, well perhaps. But I can't move closer to what I see."

"Look Flynn, just start at the beginning, tell me what's the matter and take your time. If I'm to help I need to understand as clearly as possible."

"It was a few months ago. I had a dream, a vaguely unpleasant dream which I wouldn't remember at all now if it hadn't repeated itself the next night, and then become a positive familiar. I would be dreaming the usual inconsequential nonsense just before waking in the morning when the episode would include or be partially overridden by a feature which, to put it bluntly, I wanted to get away from, but of course couldn't. It was in itself nothing ugly or nightmarish – just a shadow and –"

"May I interrupt you a moment? When did this start?"

"In June. I didn't note the date."

"No, of course one wouldn't. But had you been doing anything unusual or excessively demanding or whatever at about that time?"

"I don't think so. I was very busy with the contractors setting up the new library shop and finishing off the laundrette access that the JCR were so keen on. But that's all."

"You were saying what this thing was like?"

"Yes, but it wasn't like anything. No more than a dead tree-trunk seen in the middle distance or a blackish coat hung in dim light on the far side of a room. Very indistinct but threatening, and approaching."

"And it bothered you?"

"Oh yes. So much so that I began to set the alarm earlier and earlier to try to keep away from it, but without success."

He paused to sip sherry. It was my favourite Manzanilla and not to his taste but he didn't seem to notice. I wondered why he had chosen me as his confidant. We had an otherwise healthy minded mathematician in college – Lovebelow – who was besotted with psychoanalysis and would have delighted to spin a case history out of this sort of stuff. I suppose I was conveniently across the quadrangle, and certainly Lovebelow's endless digging for the answers he wanted to hear would have infuriated Flynn.

"Now as a medical man", he continued, "you will say that dreams are of no account." (I noted carefully what I would say as a medical man.) "Nasty dreams can generally be thwarted by abstaining from cheese or taking more exercise. I tried all that, but nothing would stop it, and the business was becoming very wearing."

"But to put it in conventional terms," I interrupted, "if it was always much the same, didn't familiarity begin to breed contempt of a sort?"

"No, rather the reverse. Like some awful dog awaiting you in a dark lane, knowing it was there made it worse. And it was getting more active. Instead of merely being there as a threat or a warning of ... I don't know how to put it ... as if I were going to be enveloped or crushed by something, it began to move closer to me. I was waking up choking or gasping, pushing it away."

"Did you still not know what it was?"

"Just a dark shape. Upright. I was quite desperate. Then the dream suddenly stopped."

"You mean you stopped dreaming altogether?"

"No, I still have waking dreams – the familiar fragments of experience. Like bits of old TV programmes appearing randomly, entirely harmless. But the shadow had gone."

"So you're all right again?"

"No." He spoke the word slowly and left it hanging in the air. I still have the strongest impression that I knew what he was about to say, although I cannot decide whether the faint tingle of anxiety I experienced was for Flynn's sanity or from some other cause. "The dream stopped two weeks ago," he said. "Since then I have seen it twice."

I sat still, waiting for him to go on, but he was fumbling in his pocket for cigarettes. I loathe tobacco smoke in my rooms. The filthy smell lingers in curtains and on one's clothes and even in one's hair. But on this occasion I didn't feel I could stop him. Instead I put a saucer on the table at his right hand to catch the ash. He blew out a long cloud of smoke with evident relief. For the briefest moment I had the irritating idea that he was enjoying himself. Then I looked at his fingers. He was ceaselessly tapping his thumb at the unsmoked cigarette.

"Where did you see it?" I asked to get him talking again.

"I was sitting in the chapel at evensong. You know how damnably ill lit the place is with those ghastly candles none of you will allow to be augmented with proper lights. I was at the back in the Fellows' pews, and it was towards the end of the service. I was thinking about something else when I became aware of some shadowy thing standing at the top of the chancel steps, about the height of a man. I knew it. But I couldn't get away, and I had enough sense to know I couldn't be harmed in a mass of undergraduates and colleagues. Obviously no one else saw it."

"Was it there for long'"

"Five or six minutes maybe."

"Could you look away from it?"

"Oh yes. It was in one place, and kept there. I looked very hard at it feeling oddly safe in the crowd. Then after the final hymn the chaplain moved in front of it to give the blessing, and it was gone."

"You're quite certain no one else saw it?"

"As certain as I can be. People would have moved or responded somehow or talked afterwards. The thing was obvious, at least to me, standing just below the communion table where the pulpit was located in the seventeenth century. No one said a word at dinner afterwards."

"Have you seen it since the chapel? When was that by the way?"

"Ten days ago. Yes I have. That's why I decided I must talk to someone."

"Go on."

"I was giving a lecture this morning. You know I use the old Wesley chapel for my Friday morning course on economic organization. I think you had to give way for me because so few turned up for your lectures last year. I was about three-quarters of the way through, when I looked up from my notes and saw what at first I took to be an unusually tall undergraduate standing by the door at the back of the hall. There was bright sunshine outside – you know what an unseasonably lovely day we had to start with – and I'd left the door at the back open to ventilate the place as the central heating had gone wrong again and was pumping out enough calories to cook a turkey. So it was difficult to see exactly. But I had to look, and when I had seen, I couldn't take my eyes off it. I must have stopped long enough to upset my audience because several of them turned round, obviously saw nothing out of the ordinary, and looked back at me. But I couldn't go on. I made some excuse. Maybe they thought I was ill. Perhaps I was."

"Maybe it was a tall undergraduate in a dark coat," I suggested archly.

"No, as they left I kept my eyes on it, and it never moved. It was still there when the hall was empty."

"It was very brave of you to stay alone."

"Not really. I was never quite alone. Tom had come in behind me to clean the board as he does between lectures. He gave me the courage to walk straight off the dais towards the thing and on out into the sunlight –"

"And there was nothing there?" I interrupted him.

"There *was* something there, but when I'd walked the length of the hall – you'll remember the Wesley Hall is about half the length of the chapel, so I was closer to it this time – I was still the same distance from what I was seeing as when I started. It wasn't an optical illusion, and it wasn't my eyesight. It was as though my visual field had a hole in it through which I could see the figure at a given distance. And when I closed my eyes, the sight was shut out just like ordinary vision. What did happen, is that when I reached the open door where I had first seen it during the lecture, there was nothing *there*, and I could see nothing unusual in the sunshine beyond. It wasn't until I got back to my rooms that I realized I was shaking like a leaf. I can't go on like this. What am I to do? I must be ill."

"Tell me more. It threatens you. It's dark. It's like a human figure. Can you go any further?"

He gazed for what seemed a long time into the fire before replying.

"I don't know if I can. There is no movement in it, but it is getting nearer to me, more directed at me – a malevolence that ... I can't help putting it this way ... that's seeking *me*." He looked up suddenly. "I can give you an idea what it's like visually, not its effect. You've seen the Epstein Lazarus in New College haven't you? Well imagine that you'd never seen it before, and you were seeing it at a distance and in very poor light, and the light was behind it. Then you look again, and it's closer to you, and darker, but you haven't moved."

As he seemed to have finished I stood up to poke the fire. The room was rather cold, but my activity was to give a few moments to consider how to handle the situation. Without extensive physical tests and observations it's a little difficult to advise an apparently sane man who is suffering from a recurring illusion. The odd feature was the particularity of the thing.

"When you saw it in the chapel and the Wesley Hall, you were taken by surprise? I mean you hadn't been consciously thinking about it?"

"Certainly not."

"Apart from sight, you haven't any other sense that it's independent of you?"

"I don't think so."

"You don't *think* so, but there is something else?"

"I'm not certain. I think it's just the blood pumping in my ears."

"What is?"

"A kind of faint drumming. Like a slow heart beat. I can hear it now, faintly."

"Quite. Look Flynn, if I'm to be of any help I must ask a few rather personal questions – in confidence of course."

"I expected you to. I hoped you would. It's the privilege of medical men. Go on. I shall not keep anything back."

"You don't ever drink much more than a glass or two of sherry and some wine at dinner do you?"

"No more than you do."

"That's what I thought. And you haven't suddenly altered the dosage in any way or tried alcohol in any unusual form – I mean in strange liqueurs or anything of that sort?"

"No."

"Is there any sort of family history, however remote or hearsay, of nervous or mental illness?"

"Not that I've ever heard of. They were mostly farmers specializing in the prosaic. In potatoes to be exact," he added with evident distaste.

"Well let's try another line. Have you been taking any drugs recently, however ordinary, legal or illegal, under prescription or not?"

"No, no, nothing," he exclaimed impatiently. "Oh well I suppose I took a couple of aspirins about two nights ago for a touch of neuralgia in my arm, and come to think of it I also had a bit of a headache."

"That was before the lecture-hall experience?"

"Yes."

"Which arm was the pain in?"

"The left."

"Are you prone to headaches, I mean before the first of these appearances?"

"No. Just a very rare one, with a cold or after sleeping too late or something like that."

"And they haven't increased in frequency recently?"

"No."

"This one you had two or three nights ago: it wasn't unusually severe or in any way odd or accompanied by pains elsewhere?"

"I don't think so. It went. I'd never have mentioned it if you hadn't specifically asked me."

"Where was it?"

"Vaguely front of the head. Nothing specific."

I was surprised how meekly he submitted to my questions. It was unlike the man. He must have been very worried indeed, and thankful to communicate anything which might help, however irritating my persistence with small details might be to him.

"Have you had any medical treatment for anything whatever in, say, the last six months?"

"Nothing, never been properly ill since I had rheumatic fever as a boy."

"Oh really? ... Well I don't suppose that's relevant. Let me rephrase the question. Is there anything you might have gone to a doctor about but in the end didn't?"

"No, I'm a pretty poor customer as far as you lot are concerned."

"So it would seem. Have you at any time recently had any sense of remoteness from your surroundings? Any sense of loftiness or detachment or unreality or dizziness?"

"Not at all. I don't go in for that sort of nonsense."

"I didn't think you did but I had to ask."

"By the way," I added casually. "Have you told anyone else about any of this?"

He hadn't.

"Well Flynn, I'll give you my advice for what it's worth" (and I think it was good advice since no concern of my own then intruded). "It's not for me to do it, but I would suggest you go to your GP and ask him for a very thorough physical check up –

blood tests, cardiograph, eyesight and brain scan. Spin any yarn you like. I doubt if there is any serious physical cause of these unpleasant appearances, if only because they are too specific and limited, but if you can establish that nothing's the matter, it will relieve your mind immensely. If something is, it can probably be dealt with. Secondly, if anything more happens, don't try to keep it to yourself. Tell me. I'm usually here in the evenings, but come at any time, and if I can help I will. And thirdly, if you need it, and it won't do you any harm, I can give you something very mild which will ensure a decent night's rest."

"Thanks, but I'm sleeping alright. No dreams. It's moved on from there. I'll be going. Thanks for listening. I'll take your advice. Good night."

He left abruptly, as if he had just remembered something important to do. When he had gone, and I had swept up the cigarette ash before it was trodden into the carpet, I sat and tried to make sense of his problem on the assumption that physical aetiology did not provide an answer. When that proved futile, I tried to return to my own work, and when that too failed I flung the whole lot down in disgust and walked across to the Senior Combination Room for some Madeira and a look at *Punch*. One of the snags with other people's problems is that when they unpack them for you to look at they leave the wrappings behind.

It was pure coincidence that brought the chaplain there at the same time. Some Christian Union people had been giving him a hard time all evening and he had at last escaped to the comparative sanity of *Private Eye* when I arrived. We didn't speak much, but I casually mentioned the lighting in the chapel. "An undergraduate, I forget who, remarked that the sanctuary was rather darker than usual. I believe he was speaking in particular about evensong a week ago past Sunday," I said.

I seemed to have scored a minor hit, for the chaplain looked quite thoughtful.

"Funny you should mention it. I never have much difficulty with the light, but on that occasion – yes I remember it well – towards the end of the service, I was reading the final collects and giving the blessing, and when I looked down I couldn't see the page at all. It didn't matter of course as I know it by heart. I thought I might have to get spectacles, but it hasn't happened again. It was just a passing aberration. I'm surprised anyone else noticed."

I too was surprised. But all it could mean was that the sanctuary was indeed darker than usual on that particular occasion. Perhaps a candle had not been lighted properly somewhere.

I saw nothing of Flynn until lunch the next day. He looked normal. Indeed he was his ordinary abrupt self as far as I could hear, and very different from the man I'd talked to the previous night.

Two hours later I was in my rooms when he came to see me: burst in would be a better description. He was a most unhealthy colour, livid with a pinkish flush at the temples and forehead, and fighting for breath. I was surprised and somewhat disconcerted. I had not expected to see him again so soon and looking so ill. "I've seen it again," he gasped.

Fortunately no one was with me to overhear, and I closed the door quickly. He was shaking like an aspen leaf. Tea had just been brought in. I poured him some and slipped in sugar, whether he liked it or not. He swilled it down as if it were cold water, the cup clattering against his teeth some of the time. I turned on the electric fire and directed it at him. After his first outburst he seemed incapable of speech.

"You're perfectly safe here," I said. "There's nothing here with us, and no one watching or listening. Tell me what's happened."

"A few minutes ago. In the Old Library. In one of the upper bays. I was looking up a reference to Ricardo." He stopped and fumbled for his cigarettes. His hands shook and he broke a match in his attempts to strike it. "I had a book open, and was standing against the wall of books that separates one bay from another – you know how it is. It was very quiet. I thought I was alone in the place, and then I felt – I don't know – that sort of prickly aware-ness – the tiny combination of silences and suspended movements, an almost insensible change of light – yes that was it, the light. I looked up and could see no one. But you know the shelves in those dividing bays have no backs to them. The books face outwards on both sides so that if you look carefully you can see over the tops of the books on each shelf into the next bay. It was there."

"What was?"

"Good god man! The thing I told you about!"

"You mean you saw it properly?"

"I saw what it was. I was as close to it as I am to you now."

"Well what is it? What did you see?"

"It's ..." he swallowed and looked hard at me as if he couldn't trust his own words or my response to them. "It's dark and cold and absorbs light. It has a hood over its head and I couldn't see its face, but it was looking at me, and I'd seen it before."

"In dreams?"

"No, for real."

I let the claim pass for the moment. "What did you do?" I asked.

"Nothing. I couldn't move. Like a nightmare. I don't think I was breathing. Then a door banged at the end – it was Bentley coming in – and I fled. I don't know what he thought. I had to get away."

"So you never looked at it properly?"

"I didn't. I couldn't. I know the thing. It's utterly absurd and dreadful. I think I'm going to die."

I had just time to say "Don't be ridiculous" before he put his face into his hands and rocked forward. I felt for an embarrassing moment that he was going to cry, but he sat up again and with his eyes focused upon the middle distance said, "It's one of the stone effigies we took up out of Challoner's graveyard."

The identification of his fixation was so prosaic, so manifestly solid and impossible, that I suffered an almost irresistible inclination to burst out laughing. Whatever medical or psychological interest this case might have had fell away in an instant. But the undeniable fact remained that Flynn was worried and frightened to an inordinate degree. With an effort I regained control of my feelings – not as difficult as it might have been since even then a deeper idea, no more than the ghost of an idea at that stage, had planted itself in my mind. But I do not believe it influenced what I then did, which seemed to be spontaneous, and common sense of a sort, although it might have involved pushing someone else to the brink, or over it.

"Look here," I said. "I think the best way to settle something like this is to face it. Let's collect the key of the crypt from your office and I'll come down with you and you'll see everything is alright and that a heap of old stones is as safe and harmless as could be."

Somewhat to my surprise, although it was in keeping with the robust haste of the man, he jumped up with great alacrity.

"Agreed. We'll go at once."

The entrance to the chapel crypt is down a narrow flight of stone steps behind a small electrical substation. As Flynn opened the door a great wave of heat and oil-fouled air swept out at us from the blackness. The boilers were for a moment silent and one could hear and see nothing except for a faint beating sound which I took to be part of the mechanism. It was years since I had been down there but I had a dim recollection of avenues of barrel-vaulted arches criss-crossing under the whole area of the chapel, all of it ill lit, filthy, and cluttered with rubbish. But Flynn had changed all that. As he clicked the switches by the door, rows of neat electric bulbs came on over the entire area showing up white-washed vaults and the vast brooding bulk of the boiler in the cen-tre, silver-painted pipes and wires passing from it to various extremities of the floor. But he hadn't succeeded in banishing all the dust, and it had eddied about on the stone flags.

"Where did you have the bits and pieces from the graveyard put?" I asked.

"Over there, behind the boiler."

"Perhaps I should lead the way?"

"No, no. It's quite alright. I understand the place. You'll fall over something."

I stole a glance at Flynn. His insulting implication that I was some sort of idiot child suggested that he was either very much in command of himself again or that he had genuinely calmed down. I followed him in a slightly circuitous progress across the flag-stones while he barked out unnecessary orders to mind my feet. When he stopped I all but walked into him.

We could now see past the boiler into a corner where a num-ber of stone bits and pieces lay about on the floor. But dominat-ing the group was an upright figure. The effect was perfectly extraordinary, even, I have to admit, slightly sinister, and I was hard put to take my eyes away from it to look at Flynn. His face was registering in rapid succession, almost simultaneously, sur-prise, alarm, and perhaps anger: which was not exactly what I had expected. I looked back at the figure and we both walked slowly towards it. The thing was huge, and we stopped a respectable distance away. Indeed Flynn held my elbow.

"Don't go too close," he said quietly. "That thing looks as though it could fall at the touch of a feather. I wonder if one of the workmen told me about it and I didn't properly register what he was saying. But why on earth did they stand it up?"

"Macabre joke?" I suggested weakly.

But the thing was far from a joke. I vaguely remembered something of it, couchant on one of the tombs, with a few shabby pigeons using it as a roost. But it took on a new life in the crypt. It was about seven feet tall, blackened and gnawed away with age. The head was bowed beneath the ruins of a hood and even in the harsh light of the electric bulbs its face was an invisible darkness in the stone. The arms were folded, the hands tucked into the opposite sleeves so that no limbs were anywhere visible. Long drapes of stone ran down to where the feet should have been. The red alabaster of its surface, the area which had been uppermost when it had lain outside on the tomb, had been eroded by the rains of centuries into a mass of brownish quartz crystals, each two or three inches long, and pointing at us like dozens of sharpened fingers. It reminded me of the top of one of those spiked boxes devised by medieval cruelty for the torture of malefactors.

Leaving Flynn for a moment I edged round to one side. The back was featureless: clean stone detached from the face of the tomb. But the figure had at some stage been recumbent in the crypt. I could see its outline in the dust. The workmen must have stood it up later for some reason, but they had left no footprints. I rejoined Flynn. The place was insufferably hot and I was already sweating profusely. "Have you seen enough?" I asked.

"Yes I have. This sort of sweat house isn't exactly your style of thing is it?" I made no comment. Flynn was clearly returning to normal form. When we were out in the fresh air again and he was locking the door, he continued: "You know I'm grateful to you for having the sense to make me go and have a look down there. I must have been told about it and not registered the fact properly, and the unconscious worry appeared in my dreams and imagination. I'm going over to my office to arrange with the clerk of works to send men and ropes down there first thing tomorrow morning to lower it onto its back. It's terribly dangerous. The first inquisitive oil-delivery man who goes to have a look could easily get crushed to death. The thing must weigh a ton or more, and it's actually rocking. Did you notice?"

I hadn't.

"I'll also have to get the maintenance engineers tomorrow," he concluded. "Did you hear that knocking? Something's not right down there."

He walked off briskly and I returned to my rooms. No wonder Flynn had been upset if that was the creature in his dreams, or illusions, or fixation, or whatever jargon my colleagues would choose to employ on his behalf. But it was highly satisfactory that he had been able to explain it all so neatly to himself. Lovebelow would have been delighted with the breakthrough. It is wonderful how much ignorance can be disguised with the label "unconscious". I found myself fearing – I think it was fearing – that the disguise would not work well for Flynn later on, when darkness came.

I did not sit near him in hall – there were a lot of us at dinner that night – and we were conversing in different groups afterwards, although later, from my rooms, I happened to notice his light go out across the quadrangle at about eleven o'clock, just before the rain began.

He was not at breakfast, but this of course was of little surprise to me and of no significance to anyone else since he frequently stayed in his rooms for coffee or whatever he had. Indeed I was trying not to think about him at that stage. But as I came down the dining-hall steps into the November rain I caught sight of a group of workmen standing in the mud at the side entrance to the chapel. I stopped.

"Have you got it down safely?" I asked.

"We can't find wot 'e wants us to do," muttered old Tom, their foreman, through a mouthful of ill-fitting teeth.

"Lower to the ground that dangerous-looking statue standing in the far corner."

"There ain't one to lower." His pipe bubbled angrily with its usual malevolence.

"Well there was yesterday. I saw it myself," I said impatiently, leading the way down the steps. They followed reluctantly.

When we got to the position where I could see the stone relics, I was brought to an abrupt halt. The statue was indeed there, but it now lay – quite harmlessly and astonishingly enough unbroken – on its face. A few fragments of quartz had spurted out onto the flagstones at the impact. Nothing moved and the beating of the machinery or whatever it was had fallen silent.

"It must have overbalanced in the night," I said, and left before anyone could reply or see my face.

I went straight for Flynn's staircase at a near run – anyway fast enough to make several people look at me. It was a foolish and sudden impulse which I had later to explain. Luckily both his bedmaker and Dick, the college butler, were on the bottom landing, so I had witnesses.

"Have you seen Mr Flynn this morning?"

"No sir, I generally wait until he comes out."

"Well come up with me now. He may be ill. Bring your keys. And

Dick, will you come as well. We may need your help. He wasn't well yesterday."

Flynn's set was on the top floor and I was out of breath by the time we got there.

"Shall we knock or go straight in sir?" asked Mrs Stubbs. "'E never locks 'is door."

There had been time on the way across, and while climbing the staircase, for me to recover from the stange panic occasioned by the fallen statue. After all, I had been acting on the premiss that the college was more peaceful before Flynn came, and I knew that everyone would be in agreement about his successor. It would be wise, I concluded, to proceed as planned: as if I believed he was alive and as well as what I surmised to be his heart condition would permit.

"We'll knock," I said. "But he doesn't always hear. Give me your keys Mrs Stubbs."

Using the keys as a knocker I beat loudly and rhythmically upon the oak.

"Maybe 'e can't 'ear yer," the bed-maker whispered. I agreed, and struck the door again, one followed by two repeated.

"He'll know it's me. It's a knock we understand," I said by way of explanation. But I was smiling to myself.

"We had better go in," I said at length. "He would surely have heard us after all that." I turned the handle and was genuinely surprised to find it locked.

Mrs Stubbs took a few seconds to identify the right key since I had inadvertently shuffled the bunch when knocking. In the pause I experienced a curious inclination to giggle. My mother would have said I was over excited.

The oak opened outwards; the inner door away from us. But it stuck on something on the floor. With a lot of effort and help

126

from Dick the two of us managed to push it open. Someone must have carried a lump of mud and stones up on their shoes, and the mixture had become wedged between the foot of the inner door and the floorboards as we tried to get in.

There was no sign of him in the drawing-room and everything was in the somewhat bleak order that Flynn liked. Mrs Stubbs pulled back the curtains while Dick and I crossed to the bedroom door. I tapped as before, but more gently this time. There was no response. I opened the door and switched on the light, moving in such a way that Dick could see what was there as easily as I could. Flynn was in bed. He was lying on his back, gazing at the ceiling, his face contorted into a most peculiar expression whose precise character I do not care to remember. Dick later, and somewhat fancifully, described it as horror; but it could just as easily have been the result of a sudden killing pain. The bedclothes were ravelled – as though he had been moving violently. There was nothing we could do. It caused me no surprise that I was later able to agree with the pathologist's opinion that he had died about six hours before we found him.

There was necessarily a post mortem. It revealed, as I suspected, the slight heart abnormality typically associated with rheumatic fever and this, together with the help of an edited report of my quasi consultation, and some inconclusive evidence of a heart attack, was sufficient to identify the cause of death. Indeed heart failure was the only ascertainable cause since the adrenaline secreted during acute fear decays beyond trace within an hour or so. The only abnormal thing about the body was on the chest and abdomen where a number of small depressions could be seen in the flesh without laceration or contusion: not really injuries at all in any accepted sense. I have to say these puzzle me, although I suspect a case of mind-imposed stigmata of the sort that certain Christian enthusiasts can rather dramatically inflict upon themselves. Certainly neither the marks nor the lump of mud inside the door played any part in my little joke. Flynn's habit of leaving his door unlocked at night – I believe he was afraid of fire – positively enticed someone to walk in suitably cloaked and stand at the foot of his bed in the small hours. My great fear was looking ridiculous, and there had indeed been a risk. But a doctor can always say that he is concerned about a patient. Especially if he hears a cry across the quadrangle coming from the general direction of the patient's room. I suppose the Yale-type lock must have slipped off its catch somehow. But that too is puzzling, unless another visitor came.

[The MS of the above was found among its author's papers after his death. Since he had no relatives, and the college was his sole beneficiary, it has advisedly remained unpublished for a considerable number of years. The modern reader may be interested to know that the good doctor succeeded Flynn as Bursar, and that he caused Challoner's graveyard to be beautifully reconstructed. His own ashes were in due course interred there behind a plaque on the chapel's wall. The plaque commemorates his degrees and services to medicine, and concludes with his virtues, among them being "the beloved physician" who ministered to the needs of the college for more than fifty years.]

Blindburn

I am lost to peace, I am lost to grace,
I am lost to all that's beneath the sun;
I have lost my way in the dead o' night
And the gates of Heaven I have never won.

Old Ballad

"The trouble with being middle aged is that surprise has gone out of the world. Christmas is a repetition of things too familiar. The endless cycle of nature begins anew ..."

Our hostess caught my eye nervously. Cleghorn as a postprandial philosopher was dangerous. His quiver of laboured unoriginality was evidently about to be released at us over the port and claret.

"Perhaps," she said brightly, "perhaps Professor Wishart could surprise us with a story?"

I had been primed for the invitation should the need for it arise at the end of dinner.

"I fear most of my stories are rather long and uninteresting," I said.

The polite murmur of dissent was marred only by the audible agreement of my wife several places along the table.

"However," I continued resolutely, "there was once something, long ago now, which still worries me at times. It has the minor disadvantage of being true, which rather limits the imagination, but that apart, I have an idea there is a story in it somewhere although I have never made sense of it. Someone might say that the boundaries were adjusted for a moment. Then again there's always the sceptic who laughs about flights of fancy. I could easily play the sceptic myself. But there would be no laughter."

The company sat back, complacent in their captivity, some of the weaker spirits evidently settling themselves so that a sudden onset of sleep would not result in their toppling face first into the fruit and nuts.

It was many years ago, towards the end of December. I'd only been up at Oxford for a term, and with the enthusiasm of youth I'd somehow persuaded three other men from my college to come climbing during the vacation. The obligatory family Christmas had worked its way through turkey and paper hats, and squabbles with my father and elder sister, and with a sense of relief I boarded the overnight sleeper from Euston – on the evening of the twenty-seventh I think it must have been. Relief was less to the fore when I got off the train at eight the next morning. The platform of the desolate little station half way between Perth and Inverness was still almost dark. A misty rain fell thickly. Beyond the station, a row of unlit cottages and a hotel, closed for the winter, straggled along a road which was to become the A9, but was then little more than a byway for local traffic that couldn't use the railway.

The youth hostel we'd selected as our base camp could only be reached on foot. It stood alone, some six or seven miles from the village and the nearest road, almost at the head of a narrow loch which lay to the north-west. However the warden lived close to the station, and it was necessary to book in and collect the key at his cottage before proceeding: or so the SYHA handbook informed us. None of us had been there before.

He was not pleased to see me. Wardens, he made it clear, were not paid to be disturbed at that hour. The drawn curtains and suggestion of stale whisky underscored his displeasure. I explained I had come off the Inverness train and was the first of the party, the other three being booked to join me two nights later. He reluctantly opened the door into a small lobby. The yellowing wallpaper and tired rugs smelt faintly of damp wool and food. I signed the overnight book and paid him whatever it was – two shillings and threepence a night I think. The key, he said, was already at the hostel "wi' twa young laddies". He stamped my YHA card and was in the act of handing it back when he hesitated, staring at the passport photograph it contained.

"That's a bonny likeness," he said. And then, "I dinna think the likes o' yersel' will need ony directions frae me."

I explained I had never been there before and didn't know the district, despite having been born in Aberdeen.

He looked up sharply at me with pale, rheumy eyes and I felt he was about to say something about me or my name, but instead, after a pause, he just gave directions. "Go past the station. Turn left ower the auld brig. Follow the path across the heather by the electricity posts and along the north shore of the loch. It's six mile. The other laddies are leaving tomorrow so you'll be by yersel' for the night. Hae ye matches and a candle? The electricity isn'a to be relied on."

I said I had matches, a torch, candles and a Primus stove, as well as plenty of provisions.

"Weel, mind yersel' and if ye are in trouble in the dark, bide still until the dawn. The Blindburn's no a couthie place in the night, even for those that can see." Then he added defiantly, "I want no rescue work this season. If ye need onything, Alan Wishart, ye must come back for it – by day."

The unexpected emphatic use of my name was a little intimidating, but it occurred to me that he did it with everyone to emphasize that he knew who was there if any damage was done. His old, pinched, unshaven face glowered after me in the half dark of the winter dawn as I set out in the rain to look for the little peaty track to the loch. I was beginning to regret very much that the others would not be arriving till the 30th. But the die was cast, and I had cast it, and I was still to learn my limits.

The hostel was not the usual shooting-lodge or mansion abandoned to the use of the decently poor or strenuously healthy. It was a mean little stone cottage, with an open wooden porch, a door in the middle, and a single window either side. At the back, dark scree slopes climbed steeply into the low cloud that hung over everything. A small burn splashed past the side of the bothy and disappeared into stony turf some yards below. Hence, I presumed, "Blindburn" – the name on the Ordnance Survey map. In the foreground, a hundred yards or so of nasty-looking peat hags lay between cottage and loch. As I approached the door, I saw the boots of the "twa laddies" tucked in under narrow benches on either side of the porch. Evidently they were not scampering about on the high hills in the rain. "Softies," I thought, with all the easy arrogance of an Oxford Blue, although I had no more to my own credit than rowing once in the Christ Church regatta.

The porch opened directly into a small common room with a

trestle table and some kitchen chairs in the middle. A few orange boxes had been tacked together on one wall to form partitioned shelves, and a black stove stood at the rear of the room for cooking and heating. The only other room, "dormitory" is too grand a word, opened off to the right. It was slightly smaller, and smelt of musty pine and varnish like an old Methodist chapel. In it were four bunks of regulation sparseness – narrow iron things, with one berth above and one below. The SYHA handbook was very emphatic that there were sleeping places for only eight *males*. Like the common room, the single window looked out to the front, across the peat hags to the loch. There was no running water, except the burn, and no other accommodation, except for an unpleasant earth closet standing by itself behind the cottage. It had to be reached by going out of the front door and round the side. Fortunately the young have elastic capacities!

By the time I arrived, the rain had diminished to a drizzle, and I was thankful to find the stove lit and two long-boned youths sitting beside it. I never learnt their full names. They were just Len and Eric, decent fellows despite their endless talk about football stars and skiffle groups. They seemed genuinely pleased to see me, and were as openly curious about Oxford and my accent as I was invincibly ignorant about Mansfield Town and theirs. I was glad of their company. But it was, I suppose, their company which set the scene for what I experienced after they had gone.

I am, and have always been, untroubled by ordinary loneliness – empty houses and silent hills do not bother me nearly as much as a cold bed or doubts about the quality of the next meal. But I was, and I hope I still am, sensitive to the moods of other people, and as the early twilight began to close in – I should perhaps say we had all tried a walk earlier, but the low clouds made it dangerous and useless to do any climbing – as darkness fell, it was born in on me that both boys (they might have been a couple of years younger than I was at the time) were nervous. I can only say they kept very close together, and seemed peculiarly loath to let me out of sight. They would come with me on some excuse if I went to the bedroom, or outside with me to look at the weather. And they talked too much. I don't mean like people who chatter and are happy; but more like those who talk eagerly and continuously to stop something being said or heard. I didn't have the sense to ask them what was the matter. Instead I made things worse by deliberately and slightly mischievously playing up the situation. I brought the talk round to stories about empty houses and things that might have happened in hidden places. I wouldn't do it now. In the wrong situation it can give some people a heightened alertness to sound and movement which becomes genuinely frightening. One listens, and one hears – all very entertaining in a warm room in company after a good dinner (I caught my hostess's eye) but not so welcome when there are only three of you, and empty darkness for many miles.

I turned in early, and they followed with sheep-like sociability which ought to have been irritating but was somehow welcome. It seemed quite sensible that none of us should linger by the dying stove; but no reason was given or discussed. For a long while we lay talking, laughing nervously at a bunk that creaked somewhere even when no one would admit to moving. I was the first in bed, but I believe the last asleep, and my final impression – I may have been asleep already and partly wakened in the night – was of someone moving about and crying. If I had been properly awake I would have been embarrassed, and just possibly I'd have done something about it. As it was, I was too fuddled and cosy with sleep to be pulled back into consciousness. If I thought at all, I must have presumed it was one of the boys. But in the morning I remembered it more like a dream than something heard. I didn't say anything.

The morning was bitterly cold. A hard frost, clear skies and a dry north-east wind had replaced the Atlantic fret of the previous day. For a while I lay inside my sleeping-bag fortified by several layers of thin youth hostel blankets which would have been equally at home in a police cell or a mortuary. I tried in vain to shrink into the ever-retreating pool of warmth somewhere in the middle of the bunk. I think the others were doing the same. In the end we flapped out of bed like rocketing pheasants, and dressed with furious speed.

The boys were leaving that morning, and we walked the long path back to Badenoch Station together: they to catch the mid-day train south, I to fetch half a hundredweight of coke from the yard at the station. I wouldn't carry it *now* to save my life, but then it seemed a small price to pay for warmth, and for light, although I was not thinking of that at the time.

As they left, they were both full of cheerful banter about the prospects for my coming night alone. It was suddenly at the tip of my tongue to ask if they had heard anything unusual the previous night. But the moment passed. A man of twenty-one is more afraid of stumbling on another man's tears than he is of physical injury. But as their train started to move, Eric rather deliberately called me from their compartment window, as if he had been saving it until I couldn't question him further. His voice, and the sight of him were disappearing in a cloud of steam and engine smoke as the train pulled into a cutting beyond the deserted platform. He called, "Don't worry. There's nothing there," or something like that. I returned slowly, along the shores of the loch, reluctantly aware that I did not want to be alone that night.

The darkness came on quickly despite the clear skies, and the soggy turf near the bothy was crisp with the onset of frost by the time I got back. I lit the stove with dry heather, and tried to make the place cosy, but without much success. The piteous supply of electricity which hobbled up from the village along a row of rickety posts which I had followed twice that day was only sufficient for a comfortless glow in the middle of the common room and the same in the dormitory. Even the candle on the table gave a better light for reading. I looked out at about seven o'clock. It was very still, and less cold. The sky must have been overcast for I could see no stars. The only sound was the far away roar of wind and falling water in the mountains, and the more distinct splashing of the Blindburn near at hand. It felt like snow, which had not been forecast when I spoke to the men at the station coalyard, and snow carried with it the worry that I might be isolated from the friends who were to arrive at Badenoch the next day.

I shut the door, but apparently not properly, because it began to rattle against the worn snib as a thin wind picked up while I was cooking supper. It was then that I discovered the key was missing. No one could be there to lock out, but the unlocked door gave an unpleasant sense of insecurity. I jammed a rucksack against it in a first attempt to get some peace, and although it stopped the movement at that point, it gave no feeling of safety.

As I sat there later in the evening, at the behest of my distant tutor, trying to concentrate on some now-forgotten economic text, I was continually diverted by sounds in the bothy which eluded my hearing when I tried to attend to them, and movements – perhaps they were shadows from the candle – which I could never quite catch with the eye. I was not exactly frightened, but I was beginning to dread the thought of moving into the unlit room with the empty bunks I would not be able to see. And I would loose control of the common room with its door to things outside. Imagination, I told myself. Imagination fortified by being alone. But telling yourself this doesn't help. Then a new draught started to rattle the dormitory door, at first almost imperceptibly, and then more persistently. In a flurry of noisy movement I flung it open, dragged one of the bunks into the common room, closed the door again and stuck the back of a chair under the handle, all the time feeling the fool that I was, for no one could have been in the other room and nothing could have threatened me in it. I made up the stove with ruthless disregard for the fuel supply before securing the window. It was supposed to be covered by a mean little pull-down blind – goodness knows why they bothered out there – but the blind stuck halfway, and fixing one of the blankets across the recess of the window was the only thing that gave some relief from the feeling that one could be seen without seeing. Heavy snowflakes swirled past, scratching like soft fingernails at the glass.

I sat down and again tried to read. But concentration was impossible. I was still trying to hear something distinct from the background swish of snow and wind and water. I paced around the room. I made up the stove even more generously and sat with my back to it. But it was no good. Some sharpness of the senses or some unnatural alertness had let loose things which could not be brought under control. It was ten o'clock. I kicked off my shoes, got into the sleeping-bag on the top bunk more or less still dressed, and pulled the blankets up to my chin. I ought to have been hot. I got colder. The low-voltage bulb burned dimly in the brown ceiling, and a length of candle remained lit on the table. You see, all my reason and understanding and boyish strength said I was alone and safe. But my senses told me I was not. And yet they told me nothing I could get hold of. The hot orange glow from the stove was an ally. The wind and cold were not.

For a long time I remained awake and acutely alert, afraid not to listen, and afraid that by listening I would indeed hear something. All the while I lay on my back in order to see as much of the room as possible. Nature is, however, very strong and my body was tired by the six-mile haul back from the village with the coke. Nothing moved. Nothing changed. An overactive attention to one's surroundings cannot be indefinitely prolonged when there is nothing to focus on. There was an interval of time, more pronounced than on the first night, of which I was not conscious. Out of it I emerged slowly from the insistent pricking of acute cold. I shrank into myself, but the cold followed like snow blowing into a rabbit's burrow. I opened my eyes to darkness.

The electric light had gone. But the warden had warned that it could fail. There was no candle. It must have burnt out. I rolled my eyes sideways. There was no light from the stove. It was not merely dark. There was only void and icy space with something terrible moving in it. It may now sound absurd, but my immediate, paralyzing fear was not the thing in the room with me, but that I had gone blind – blackened out from the world by some sudden and appalling physical stroke. I knew, I absolutely knew, the terror of being sightless. Then, out in the darkness, came a distinct sound. The door-latch rattled. Something or someone was at the door. The latch rattled again, followed by the perfectly audible clash of the door shutting. It was impossible. No one could be there to go out on such a night. No one could have come up from Badenoch in the dark of the snow storm. But as in a dream, I believed. What broke the spell was feeling the hard lump of the torch under the coat I was using as a pillow. I fumbled for it. Light! Please gods, let there be light! The beam cut across the room. Both doors were shut as I had left them. The candle was reduced to a pool of its own wax. Nothing had been moved. I fell out of the bunk. The place was empty. But in my confusion I thought that some poor wretch had gone out into the cold. I could hear crying, something human beyond the howling of the storm. My rucksack was still wedged against the door. I tore it away. The door instantly blew tight against the snib. When I opened it, snowflakes flew in like a cloud of white dancing flies in the torch light. Someone was crying. I had no doubt of it now. The noise was receding into the darkness and as I stood there hesitating, it was gone. I shouted. I called. I put on my boots to go out and search. I waved my torch and called. But some practical spark of sanity, or perhaps it was the words of the warden, or the boy in the departing train, said that it was not real, not now, and that I too would be lost forever in the cold if I followed. The door banged. I felt for the latch, really blinded by the snow this time. As I barred the door again with my rucksack, my feeling was no longer panic terror of I knew not what, but an utterly inexplicable pity and sadness for the lost one who had stumbled out into the darkness that would never be lighted again, or filled with the warmth of human company. I cannot understand what happened. Fear was replaced with compassion. It was very strange.

There is a little more to tell. The candle was easily relighted after the wax had been scraped away to release the wick. The rest of the night was wearisome but nothing more. I drank coffee, wrapped up in all the blankets I could find, and sat at the table waiting for the dawn.

The next day the others succeeded in battling up from the station through quite deep drifts. They had seen the electricity posts down in one place. There was, of course, no trace of anyone outside the bothy when I was able to look, not that I really expected there to be. I said nothing about my experience to my friends, and it was perfectly obvious they sensed nothing strange about the place at any time. Neither did I. The moment, whatever it was, had passed, and what remained was empty and ordinary. But I still retain the almost entirely irrational conviction that when I woke I was blind; and that I could not have seen in those first moments had there been light to see, and that in that blindness I somehow shared an experience with another human being, for whom I felt first fear, then pity. I say *almost* entirely irrational conviction because when I looked at the stove after giving up my attempt at an expedition outside, it was still shedding its warm orange light on floor and ceiling. It had never been out, and there was no possibility of not seeing this from my position in the bunk. I put the matter to the test that very night. That's all.

I sat back from the table, aware that the narrative had not gone as well as I had hoped. Truth is usually less exciting than fiction. Giles was noisily asleep. Elizabeth Farmiloe was gallantly propping up half-shut eyelids. I glanced apprehensively at the other guests. Either my story or the claret had taken its toll. Then I saw Cleghorn. He was wide awake and staring at me as if I had jumped fully formed out of a Christmas cracker. His vast jaw, which always seemed to be winched up and down several times before he began to speak, gave warning of impending judgment. I steeled myself for a sermon.

"And you mean you have lived all these years without having the spirit to ask what it all meant?" he said.

"I don't know what you think I should have done," I replied rather stiffly. "Youth hostels don't exactly encourage psychical research or metaphysical speculation, and I have never been back."

"Why man, you could have told the warden!"

"There would have been no point. Anyway, have you ever tried revealing your private imaginings to a cantankerous, hung-over Scotsman on the 2nd of January?"

"Yes, I have," he said harshly. "The warden was my father. And because you were too timid to ask or tell, he went to his grave, God rest his soul, ignorant of what had put an end to the wandering spirit of poor Jeany Wishart."

It was my turn to stare at him, voiceless on the instant with embarrassment and surprise. But our hostess, evidently wishing to pour oil on troubled waters, interrupted.

"Perhaps, Alan," she said, "Dr Cleghorn can add to your story. I'm sure he could explain – before we all welcome in the New Year."

For a moment or two Cleghorn held back, and I had leisure to wish fervently that I had put things differently in describing the warden. But how could I have anticipated such a mischance? Then his jaw began to work again.

"I do not know that I should satisfy your curiosity," he began. "But since the hand of God has brought us together, and since you have inadvertently belittled my father's name, I think for his sake you should know the truth. Before the cottage was a hostel, when my father was a small boy, it had been for years the home of one Jeany Wishart – yes Wishart was the name. Are you surprised, Alan, that he was struck by *your* name turning up so aptly at the anniversary? She was old and frail, but she must have known every stick and stone about the place, and somehow lived out there by herself as the very old may live in a place they know well, though they will die if you move them. Then came the great storm. It may have been the snow that confused her. At any rate, when the young men from Badenoch got through some days later in the New Year, they found her body in the snow a few yards beyond the door. She was dressed in nothing but a shift. The door was latched behind her. They brought back her body, and it is buried in the kirkyard."

Cleghorn paused. Someone murmured, "Go on."

"The cottage lay empty for years and years, and then along came the new hikers, and it was patched up as a hostel. Gradually stories began to be told. Odd stories, about young climbers who would never go back there, or robust men who would up and depart at most extraordinary hours. Then suddenly it all stopped, about the time you were there, Alan, and the cottage became as normal as a postbox."

He turned to our hostess. "You will draw your own conclusions," he said. "But it is a most extraordinary thing." And then to me, "There are more things in heaven and earth than are dreamed of in your philosophy, Alan. Perhaps your compassion for the poor soul released her – for I am sure now you were the last of the many who heard her going out – and for that kindness I forgive you your inadvertent hard words about my father. You see he cared about her very much, my grandfather ... but that's an older story and nothing to the purpose."

He smiled at me, that kind smile that was more healing than all his medicines. "He did drink more than was good for him when he was old. Maybe it's the best way."

His face became serious again. "But it is an extraordinary thing. You see, for many years before her death, Jeany Wishart was completely blind."

Vanitas Vanitatum

The sky is grey, my hands are cold,
A headache wanders round my brain,
And I must dine tonight again.

The Don

Canon Judkins had lived many scholarly years in St Alban Hall in one of England's ancient universities. He was respected, wise, old and eccentric. The respect was due to his age, and his age to the inheritance of a robust constitution from an agrarian grandmother whose earthy talents had somehow slipped through the exclusive net of the Judkins' forebears. His wisdom was real, and had grown in proportion to the disappointments with which life had afflicted him. But his eccentricity was feigned as a means of allowing him the indulgence of his whims without forfeiting the goodwill of his neighbours. The Canon had learnt early in life that where oddity was expected much else would be tolerated.

For many years he had inhabited a warren of book-strewn rooms on the first floor of the staircase which had been built as a penance by Henry IV and which had been used ever since to house those whose political, social, artistic or sporting temperaments rendered them unfit for occupation of rooms nearer to the master's lodgings in the opposite corner of the quadrangle. Accordingly the staircase had housed for four hundred years a succession of roysterers and cavaliers, Jacobites and gentlemen, oarsmen and revolutionaries, and, for fifty-seven years of scholarly quietness, Canon Judkins.

In his earlier days he had laughed and loved, dined and talked, prayed and preached his way into mature manhood. Then an affair of the heart had convinced him of the instability of woman and the need for a life devoted to higher things of the mind. Since then he had only talked and worked. His talk was renowned, and was reputed to stand second only to McDowell's of Dublin and Bowra's of Oxford, but his work was as yet only a promised land. Everyone in his college and most of those in the university knew of the lifetime of scholarship which the Canon had devoted to his *History of the Decay of Christianity in Western Europe.* He had read in libraries throughout the civilized world and beyond. He had taken notes and followed references and pondered arguments and discussed sources. His rooms were filled with the product of his labours. Decades of files and writings, notes and observations, jottings and paragraphs lay everywhere about, and on his desk a great pile of manuscript slowly grew, and faded with the years.

For longer than anyone could remember he had assiduously isolated himself in his rooms between two o'clock and six o'clock every weekday afternoon writing and working. As he advanced in years the world had come to understand that the great work had also advanced, until, in his eightieth year he was intent upon the final chapter in which the learning of a Gibbon and the acumen of a Hume would combine to draw together all the threads of argument and all the data in his grand design.

In summer he worked with his back to the window until the afternoon shadows began to lengthen towards evening when he would rise and robe himself and go down to the chapel to wait upon the earthy observances of his god. In winter he would sit with his back to the fire until twilight and the footsteps of the young men in his staircase reminded him that it would be appropriate to light the lamp and stir the fire. In the evenings after dinner he would sometimes entertain undergraduates or fellows of the college, but his conversation was never of himself in the manner of the very young or very old. It concerned always the world beyond the confines of his study and the interests of his academic life. If asked about his work he would reply that it was progressing well although not as quickly as he would have wished.

In his eighty-first winter he worked more slowly, for his task was hard, and he was near to the end. His hand moved more laboriously over the paper and his head was inclined to slip down on to his chest. When he raised it again, time had unaccountably passed in the stillness of his room. In the quadrangle beyond his window the men would be returning from the river. He knew they must be there although he could no longer see them distinctly past the stone mullions. All he could see was the monk seated by the fountain – the one who had been there for a number of afternoons past and who occasionally looked up at him from beneath a black cowl which concealed the face. He was sometimes inclined to ask the visitor to come up to his rooms but always decided to wait for a little longer.

He looked down at his hands. They were stiff and insensitive. Hands, he reflected, which had once been careless and beautiful, artful in love, strong in life. His eyes closed. "Oh my sweet love, what have I done for thee in all my days," he murmured to himself. He sighed and then read again the last sentence he had written. "There is one alone, and there is not a second; yea, he hath neither child nor brother: yet is there no end of all his labour." The writing was not like his own, and the sentence bore no relation to the one preceding it. He read it over again carefully and then scored it out. As he did so he became aware that he was not alone in the room.

No living thing had disturbed him during the afternoon for as long as he could remember. He sat perfectly still with his back to the fire looking out of the window. The figure was no longer by the fountain.

"Must I speak with you?" he said at length.

"Yes," said the Visitor.

"What then do you want?"

"What have you for me?"

"This," said the Canon laying his hand on the great manuscript at his left hand.

"What has it cost you?"

"A lifetime."

"And what else?"

"Society, travel, preference in the Church, children, family, and the tender love of a woman."

"So you remember?" said the voice.

"Yes, I remember" said the Canon.

"And why did you give up all this?"

"Because of my work."

"Because you were afraid of life," contradicted the Visitor. "What is your work worth?"

"I am an old man," said the Canon. "Have done with me. It is finished."

"But for whom have you laboured, and for whom have you

bereft your soul of good?" persisted the Voice. "Two are better than one; because they have a good reward for their labour. But for him that is alone when he falls ..."

"Leave me!" interrupted the Canon.

"I am waiting for you," said the Visitor politely.

"As you wish" said the Canon. He turned his chair slowly round towards the fire. A soft warm flame played over the fading coals. "Have mercy upon me, O Lord, for I am weak and my soul is sore vexed," he murmured. His head sunk upon his chest, and he smiled wistfully into the fire for the thought of the love he had lost and the fame he would never have.

Mrs Arlingham gazed out at the sunlit quadrangle. It was a fine day for early December but there were touches of frost in the shadows by the Canon's staircase. Oh god, what a bore term had been! There were times when the cloistered living, the parties and dinners, the endless reforming committees and the essential leisure of college life bored her exquisitely. It simply refused to allow itself to be organized by her talents, and as wife of the Master she felt she had a right to organize everything. But worse than that, it was so repetitive.

Soon the men would be returning from afternoon walks or from rugby or rowing. The quadrangle would tinkle with the sound of a hundred tea spoons. The sportsmen would discuss form and style, bladework and ball control; and they would do it all in such minute detail and with such profound concern. The intellectuals would talk endless nothings (with limitless sincerity) about morality and power structures, commitment, relevance, representation and whatever other humourless abstracts were current fashion.

If Mrs Arlingham had at that moment been asked, she would have denounced the whole way of life as an infinite tediousness, a repetitive round of repetitive years. But even as she answered, her bee-like mind would have been threading its way in and out of the college rooms criticizing, fussing, reforming. Her attention might have been caught, as it was now, by the Canon's staircase.

"*Dear* Canon Judkins," she thought. "It *will* be sad when he leaves us. But how useful his rooms will be with new partitions installed and electricity and so on!" Her husband, she knew, was counting on at least seven new undergraduate bedsits in the area which at present housed the old man so uneconomically.

She was about to go for afternoon tea when a figure by the fountain caught her eye. Surely it wasn't an undergraduate. It seemed to be wearing a long dark gown, or a cloak of some kind, over its unpleasantly thin body. Why wouldn't it look up instead of keeping its head turned away from her in that irritating manner? She watched as the figure moved towards the Canon's staircase. She waited, curiously relieved that she had not seen its face but still inquisitive to know more. The Visitor was bound to emerge again so that she could see who it was, for the Canon never admitted anyone between precisely two and precisely six o'clock, and such a scarecrow could scarcely be visiting one of the undergraduates. But Mrs Arlingham's vigil went unrewarded, and the call of afternoon tea drew her from the window. Possibly it was one of the monks attached to the Roman Catholic chaplaincy she thought. But it irritated her to know that someone could entertain such an unusual-looking person in her college without her knowing who it was. She knew everyone, and *everyone* in the university knew her. Sooner or later she would meet him she reassured herself ... preferably in company with other people.

Her thoughts were interrupted by the arrival of Dr Arlingham, dry after the afternoon's committees. He was a man much in tune with the times: a researcher and administrator whose slim contributions to the *Journal of Statistics* had been widely acclaimed. He had himself been responsible for the triumphant reform of the entrance scholarships which had redirected the prizes from Greek and Theology to Economics and Computer Science, and his name was widely canvassed as the future vice chancellor of an emerging university. He sat down beside his wife.

It was after dinner before anyone looked for the Canon. His scout had gone up to his rooms to wash the tea things. When he found the outer door locked he had knocked several times at the porch. On failing to gain admittance he had raised the alarm. When the porter had brought the key they found him seated by the fire half facing towards the door, his head sunk on his chest, his eyes closed and a quiet, faint smile on his lips. In his hand he still held a pen, and on his desk lay the great manuscript which was eventually delivered to the Master of the College, for Canon Judkins had no heirs.

"Yes, it was as we all thought," the Master said to his wife one afternoon some weeks later. "It began well and then petered out into a vast array of notes and jottings. He hadn't touched it for years. He hadn't the capacity for that sort of work. Anyway scholarship on that scale went out with Murray and died with Toynbee. I suppose he really was somewhat of a liability around the place with his addiction to old forms of prayer in the chapel and so on. But the men seemed to like him. When his rooms are modernized they will be very useful for the first intake of women freshmen."

"*Vanitas Vanitatis*, all is vanity" he added, inexactly, and with deep resignation, busying himself once more with the "Comprehensive Report on Faculty Structures" which had been so long on his desk, and which would initiate such durable and educationally significant reforms when published.

The Dublin Epictetus

Like one, that on a lonesome road
Doth walk in fear and dread,
And having once turned round walks on,
And turns no more his head;
Because he knows, a frightful fiend
Doth close behind him tread.

Coleridge, Ancient Mariner

The manuscript from which this narrative is taken formed part
of the estate of my grandfather, David Ross of Straloch, who
at the time of the events described was a professor at the college
at Aberdeen. It has been in the possession of our family for most
of the present century and is here printed for the first time. As
editor I have made it my business to see that what Professor Ross
wrote is reproduced without addition or subtraction. The intrin-
sic oddness, the incomplete inferences, and the unsubstantiated
individuality of the narrative may lead the reader to ask if my
grandfather was ever mentally disturbed in any way. I can only say
that, apart from the evidence of the text itself, all reports of him

speak of a prosaic, sane, unimaginative man, temperate in his habits and moderate in his opinions. I might add, for what it is worth, that he was an elder of the Church of Scotland. The scene is at first Aberdeenshire and then Dublin. My grandfather's narrative follows.

The volume came into my possession along with others from the library of my uncle, John Forbes; or at least I found it among his books. (The reason for my slight hesitation in the matter will shortly become apparent.) The whole collection lay throughout the summer in a lumber-room at the top of my house. It was, however, not until late October that I felt any inclination to bring the somewhat shabby volumes down to my own small library for examination. They were mostly dull stuff: collections of sermons which had contributed little to the learning and nothing to the piety of the world, or sets of novels which posterity had been charitable enough to forget. But occasionally volumes came to light which were of value or interest. These I kept. The rest were set aside for removal to a second-hand book stall at the Aberdeen market.

I had almost completed the sorting and was just shuffling together a worthless collection of old bound copies of *Temple Bar*, when I came across an octavo edition of Elizabeth Carter's celebrated translation of the works of Epictetus. What initially caught my attention was the binding. It was perfect eighteenth-century calf with tooled spine and labels, but quite unusually dark, almost black. I have never seen anything like it from its period. The effect was at first striking, and then mildly unpleasant. I turned it over several times in my hands before opening it. When I did so I discovered, not a London reprint, with reduced margins, of the splendid 1758 quarto as I had expected, but something much more interesting: a subscription edition printed in Dublin in 1759. But I was a little saddened, if not altogether surprised, to discover no trace of the Forbes bookplate. Indeed I could not imagine what my uncle – who was more familiar with horses than books, and more at home with farmers than scholars – could have wanted with such a volume, unless, like the sermons, it had been mere decoration. There was, however, a claim to ownership. In two places, in faded brown ink, was the library stamp of Trinity College Dublin. Now here was a mild problem. Did I have a duty to return the book? Academic good faith might say that I had, and I could not use the excuse of distance and inconvenience since by an odd chance I had accepted an invitation to give the Donnellan Lectures there in the early summer. But then again, I myself did not have a copy of Carter's Epictetus; and I at least had come by it honestly.

I was thumbing idly over the crisp white pages with this con-test of scruple and interest occupying my mind, when I found a name written into the text in long black letters. It was above the ornament on the page immediately following the dedicatory ode. For no reason at all I read aloud the words "Johannes Stearne". It was perfectly absurd, but the sound of my own voice made me look up, as if someone had spoken to me. Although it was only four o'clock in the afternoon it was already twilight and the lamps should have been lit. The room was gloomy and cheerless. Instead of ringing for Maggie to bring them in, I stirred up the fire and sat still, looking again at the hard black letters which stood out so vividly from the fading blur of the rest of the page. I recollect closing my eyes for a moment, and finding that the name was still written in the darkness of my inner eye with an unpleasant green and shimmering replica of the real letters.

When I opened my eyes the illusion was gone, and I rather hastily turned over a bulk of pages in order not to renew it. In doing so a second manuscript addition came to light. A sentence had been underlined in black ink. It read: "He has assigned to each Man a Director, his own good Genius, and committed him to his Guardianship: a Director whose Vigilance no Slumbers interrupt." But the meaning had been corrupted by an alteration. The word "good" was crossed out. Over it was written in black letters "evil"; in the margin the same hand had inscribed "*me custodit*" ["it watches me" – Ed.]. I cannot exactly identify what it was about the passage that was so disturbing. Perhaps it was the perverse negation of the noble ideas expressed. I read it several times. As I did so the room seemed to undergo a subtle alteration. My thought was that someone had opened a door. The sense of another person was for a moment so strong that I was about to turn around to see if I were indeed alone in the room when Maggie knocked and at once came in with the lamp.

"Lord preserve 's, sir!" she exclaimed. "Ye'll dee ye'sel a mischief reading by sic a darkness! There, I'll set the lamp down by ye and the auld place will maybe tak on a wee scrimp o' cheerfulness."

I was about to say something about bringing the lamp in earlier when she bustled out in a great hurry, muttering as she went, "There's nae doubt I'll need new specs, that's for sure."

Maggie had been my housekeeper ever since my wife passed on, and I am willing to tolerate her abruptness and occasional excesses of candour in the interests of securing domestic economy. But I was a little irritated, perhaps it would be more accurate to say disconcerted, by her hasty departure. Still, she had at least brought light. My attention returned to the book. Its stiff binding had caused the pages to turn back and I found myself again looking at the signature of Johannes Stearne. As I looked I was conscious of a darkening of the field of vision and of a chill at my hands as if a semi-opaque screen had been drawn across the lamp, while the fire – which still burned brightly – seemed to give out less heat. The symptom is distinctive, but for some reason I still failed to recognize its source within me despite the earlier warning. The sensation was of an outside influence. I closed the book and put it down on the table. The last few items from my uncle's collection were still on the floor. I knelt down to try to sort through them, but I now found myself shivering and unable to see properly with one eye.

The onset of megrim is very quick. Such headaches are part of my filial inheritance and I cannot understand why I did not perceive what was the matter when I had the earlier warnings. From years of evil experience I can recognize the symptoms, and I know their cure. I can only suppose they had been obscured by my concern with the book. The thing to do is to lie down in a dark room before the attack becomes intolerable. As I stumbled out of the room I glanced back. It would be false to say I saw anything out of the ordinary, but just for a moment it seemed that the lamp, which was on the far side of my chair, was casting a shadow after me longer and darker than could have been caused by anything between us. I looked again, but my vision was blurred and the patch of livid green dazzle, which would shortly extend over the whole visual field, destroyed any attempt to focus. I groped my way upstairs, calling to Maggie as I did so to snuff the lamps. She knows me well, and, good soul that she is despite her faults, asked for no explanations. The night would be vile and I knew I would waken in the morning tired, but free of pain and able to make my way to work.

The 8:20 train into Aberdeen usually takes little more than its allotted twenty-two minutes, but that day some unexplained delay at Milltimber spun out the time to a full half hour. At first I had my accustomed smoking compartment to myself, but the college librarian sometimes joins the train at Cults. He did so that day. I wished him good morning and then, for the sake of something to say, mentioned the Dublin Epictetus. Whiston is something of an historian and a specialist in eighteenth-century religious controversies, as well as being a bibliophile, but he is over short of conversation unless fed a subject, and instead of sitting at peace or reading a paper, will cower in a corner, his eyes popping out with alarm, as silent and useless as a trapped sheep. No, he did not know about any Dublin printing of Elizabeth Carter's translation. Irish publishing was a very special branch of bibliography. Yes, it might be of value to a collector in Dublin, but the market would be very restricted. Yes, he thought I ought to take it back to the library. He wondered when and how it had been taken away from Dublin. I mentioned the name of John Stearne. Whiston's interest kindled.

"There were several of that name associated with Dublin in the eighteenth century," he said. "The one you have could be the cleric – I think he finished up as Bishop of Clogher. He was the son of another of the same name who was sometime a Fellow of TCD. The son had something to do with founding the Dublin University Press, I believe."

"Was he the sort of man who would make light of keeping a college library book?"

Whiston shook his head. He had no idea of the man's character. Then he added, after a little thought, "I do remember reading somewhere that he was a dark, isolated, saturnine sort of a man. But you're going there, aren't you?"

I said I was.

"Well there's your opportunity for finding out about him. Ask

Abbott, their librarian. He's very old but he might know."

Despite my questions I really have very little taste for the histories of obscure Irish clerics. But I did not say so after Whiston's efforts at information. Our conversation was shortly interrupted by a passenger getting in at Ruthrieston, and we completed our journey in silence.

During the day I was very occupied with lectures and it was not until I was home again and in the library after tea that I gave the matter another thought. The Epictetus lay on a side-table just as I had left it and I swept away the last of my uncle's books before returning to it again. Having talked to Whiston I was now more or less compelled to take it with me in June and present it to the library – if "present" is the right word in the context. In the meantime it could stay on my own shelves. I tried it in a suitable place but its binding was far too prominent to harmonize with any of my books. Wherever I put it, the wretched thing caught one's eye in the most ugly and intrusive fashion. I would put it in a cupboard out of sight for the duration. I was just about to do so when it fell open in my hand. I had no reason to open it. One does not need reasons for opening a book. But I suppose the reason it opened where it did was that I had been looking at that page the previous night. I looked again. My recollection was that the marked passage had been limited to one sentence, but most of a paragraph was now underlined, beginning with the sentence I remembered and continuing, "So that when you have shut your Doors, and darkened your Room, remember, never to say that you are alone; for you are not: but God is within, and your Genius is within: and what need have they of Light, to see what you are doing?"

But underlining was not the end of the matter. Again, alterations had been made. Superimposed upon the word "God" were the letters "IT" done in ink, and "genius" was ruled out and "demon" written over it in Stearne's long black lettering. Now this latter was not only perverse, but childishly inaccurate. The word "daimon" in the original might have been translated as it sounds by a schoolboy in desperate straits, or even used in that sense by a patristic writer intent upon discrediting his pagan opponents – I believe even St Matthew once used it thus – but in Epictetus the notion of *evil* demon is quite out of place. I was so upset by the translation that I consulted my own edition of the Greek text and a Liddell and Scott to confirm my memory. There were no alternative readings. The word was "daimon" and in pagan use it did not imply anything about evil or devilry in one's "genius" (as Mrs Carter had so properly translated the word).

It is a commentary upon the intentness of my pursuit of this point of translation that it was not until after I had settled the matter that the oddness of my not having noticed it the previous evening struck me with full force. Of course the room had been very dark and I had been incubating an attack of megrim. The circumstances compelled me to reason that I had somehow missed it, but my reason did not carry much conviction.

I looked at the text again, holding the book close to the lamp as I did so. The underlining was all of a piece, equally strong throughout, and the alterations were equally clear. It was really unpleasant. I suppose I must have stood thus for half a minute, crouched over the lamp the better to see. I was just about to move away towards the fire, for it was a cold evening and the wind was rising, when a knock sounded at the door. Thinking it was Maggie, I called to come in but did not alter my position. I heard the door open and then a silence which continued long enough to make me turn round hastily.

To my surprise Maggie was standing in the doorway, her face a picture of startled alarm.

"Whatever is the matter?" I demanded rather sharply.

"Lord save us!" she exclaimed. "I didna ken wha it was curled up o'er the lamp like yon. It was sae dark I though ye were a bogle."

"Maggie," I said with some asperity, "what else do you expect if you give me only one lamp and I have to crowd round it like a moth at a candle? What was it you wanted?"

Maggie is rather like a fluffed-up hen when she is upset or annoyed. But she is normally a phlegmatic body, and I expected to see her feathers beginning to subside. Instead she looked nervously around the room and then said quickly, "The minister's called. He's come to see ye about the new elder o' the kirk."

"Good gracious, woman!" I exclaimed. "Show him in at once!"

As she backed out I called after her: "And Maggie – bring another lamp. We'll have at least two in here in future."

With paraffin at 1/3d a gallon one does not wish to fling it about like water. But she was quite right. The room was altogether too dark and I had no wish to risk my eyesight for the sake of a trifling economy.

When Mr Praim entered he hesitated, and instead of shaking hands as is his habit immediately said: "Mr Ross, are you well?"

I said I was as far as I could judge the matter.

"You are pale sir, and it is far from warm in here. Would you not build up the fire a little?"

I glanced at the hearth and then at Maggie, who seemed reluctant to shut the door and be gone. She is always trying to use more coal than I need, but this time she had an ally, and I was obliged to let her put on several pieces before I could decently let her go. I was still holding the Epictetus. On a sudden impulse I handed it to the minister.

"What do you think of this?" I asked. "Look at page 46."

He glanced at the title and subsequently held the book as if the poor old Stoic were an emissary of Antichrist.

"I do not like your heathen philosophers," he began in the conversational wisdom of his calling. (Mr Praim and I do not agree in all things.) Then he stopped. His face became very still. A moment later he closed the book with a snap and put it away from him onto a side-table.

"This is wickedness," he said. "I want to see no more of it."

I hastened to explain my possession of the book as best I could. I would have liked to discuss the nature of the alterations and my curious error of observation the previous night, but something warned me that the conversation would not be fruitful. Instead I concluded, "And you think those alterations are wickedness rather than the utterances of an unsound mind?"

"I know that our Saviour turned out an unclean spirit which then destroyed the swine. I do not know whether your modern science would call that curing insanity or rebuking evil. But I say to you that book is not fit to be read in a Christian house. Put it away!"

I was most surprised at his vehemence, and to humour him I immediately hid the thing at the back of a cupboard, remarking as I did so that it could stay there until I went to Dublin. Whether I really intended to let it do just that I cannot say. But I am inclined to believe that my subconscious mind had begun to associate the idea of the book with something threatening, if not actually dangerous. Be that as it may, I did not take the volume out again, and within a few weeks it was virtually forgotten in the business of the term.

During the winter months my health, or rather my spirits, seemed to sink easily into a state of depression and uneasiness which I was and am hard put to account for. I gained some respite by a brief and enjoyable visit to my son's home in Dundee over the New Year, but the malaise returned as soon as I got back. I enjoyed work and the company of work. But to return home in the evening was not the rest and relaxation it should have been.

My house had been built some forty years earlier for the substantial owner of a granite quarry. It was in the Gothic style and was normally comfortable and agreeable. But I began to feel at odds with the place. It seemed to be full of dark corners and concealed vistas – particularly on the main staircase and in the library. Spring came late, and instead of snow and crocuses we had wind and rain and overcast days. Perhaps that was at the root of my ill humour. But from whatever cause I tended to use the library less and less, and the late – almost abrupt – arrival of summer found me a constant occupant of the smaller, brighter morning-room.

My departure for Dublin, a departure to which I was much looking forward, was planned for the end of May, and by the eighteenth of that month I was busy packing my portmanteau ready to send it in advance. It is a pity that at this stage I clean forgot the Epictetus. I eventually remembered the wretched thing just as I was about to leave the house on the morning of my final departure for Dublin. I thrust it impatiently into the valise containing my papers and valuables and arrived at the station out of breath and out of humour. I had carefully calculated upon carrying the minimum weight and books are not the lightest of things.

My normal train starts from Culter and is usually standing at the platform when I arrive. But the three minutes past nine train which I took that morning comes in from Ballater, and I had to wait a few minutes. When it appeared Mr Frazer, our station master, forestalled my attempt to find a compartment by ushering me into an empty third-class smoker. He handed up my bags and then stood back holding the door open to the now empty platform.

"What is it, Mr Frazer?" I asked, somewhat mystified by his behaviour. He would never be expecting a tip from me.

He looked up at me, or rather past me into the compartment, and then said rather oddly, "I didn't see you were alone sir."

The door slammed and I heard him call after me wishes for a safe journey. A moment later the train was in motion on the first stage of my twenty-eight-hour journey to Dublin. Lest the directors of the Glasgow and South-Western Railway complain, I hasten to add that ten of those hours would be spent – I hoped pleasantly – asleep on the new turbine steamer, the *Princess Maud*, which remains overnight in Stranraer harbour before the 6 a.m. sailing.

Although it was a fine morning when I left Culter the carriage must have been standing out overnight. It was cold and damp. I let down the window to allow warm air in. But it served little purpose and I arrived at Aberdeen somewhat afraid that I was starting a chill. The express to Glasgow which Bradshaw calls "The Grampian Corridor" was, however, warm and crowded, and it gathered passengers steadily at Forfar, Perth and the other major stations. By the time we arrived at Buchanan Street, where I had to change trains and stations, I had forgotten the dismal start to the day. But I was reminded of it towards the end of the long journey down the Ayrshire coast into Wigtown. The little train gradually shed its passengers, and by the time it was calling at those isolated stations south of Girvan, it was distinctly empty. The last occupant of my compartment, an oldish woman much encumbered with coats and parcels, got out at a nowhere of a place called, I think, Glenwhilly, and I was sorry to see her go. The engine gave a few short barks and a forlorn whistle as we got going, and then moved very quietly on across a dreary expanse of brown shadowy moorland. Although it was still full daylight I felt again that unhealthy pall which had marked the start of my journey. The sun seemed to have lost its power to warm and the dank chill of the hills crept into my bones. Altogether I was extremely glad when we reached Stranraer. It was of course the town station, not the harbour: an infelicity of the railway company which would normally have irritated me immensely. But on the present occasion I was really very glad of the opportunity for a brisk walk down to the boat.

A porter took my two small cases up the gangway. The steward who checked my ticket seemed hesitant about something, and as I indicated some impatience to be allowed to proceed he said, quite unnecessarily I would have thought: "Only one person travelling, sir?"

"Of course." I spoke rather sharply. He looked up and down the gangplank behind me.

"I'm sorry, sir. I thought I saw two passengers coming up."

"A porter was just in front of me."

He still seemed mystified but contented himself with another look at my ticket.

"If you want a cabin, sir, please enquire at the purser's office."

"I already have one booked, thank you."

On reaching the office I was vexed to discover that my booking had not come through properly and that an extra 2/6d was required for a berth. Did I mind sharing with another gent? Well I did. I had no desire to be kept awake by the possibly drunken snorings of other persons, whether designated gentlemen or not. However, the question "did I mind" was entirely rhetorical since there was no other berth available, and I bowed to my fate. I need not have worried. The young clergyman slept like a boy and at least the cabin was decently warm. In some ways I was not sorry to have his company, and I suffered no more from the chill that night or on the crowded Belfast to Dublin train.

The Provost of Trinity College had done me the honour of inviting me to stay in his house, and on my arrival I was shown to a very tolerable room on the floor of bedrooms high above the great reception room. I had known the Provost well many years earlier and it was a relief to discover how little his august position and advancing age had altered his somewhat dour, earnest character. He was still serious, godly and kind, the vast physical and moral force I remembered, and he still emanated to a degree the characteristics I have met more than once in Ulstermen: that of seeing moral and political issues through eyes more confidently informed by the Almighty than is granted to other members of the human race.

After dinner I mentioned to him that I had a rather curious volume to return to the college library: about a century and a half overdue. When I explained its history as far as I knew it, he was so interested that I immediately went up to my room to fetch it from the case of papers and valuables where it had remained locked since leaving home.

It was the first time I had handled it properly since the two evenings in my library eight months earlier. I took it up carelessly, even thoughtlessly. As I did so I became abnormally conscious of the silence in the room. I was utterly remote from the world of people and horses and tram cars in the street below. The room was like a blackening mirror. I stood still, hesitating. A wisp of suspicion or fear spread and darkened in my mind like a cloud. With a rush the memory of my housekeeper's frightened face at the door fused with other things: the steward looking for my travelling companion, the minister's warning, and the cold that haunted me.

I was standing in front of the dressing-table. My eye caught a reflection in the glass above it. I cannot bring myself even now to describe what I saw, or thought I saw, at my left shoulder, but with a cry of horror I fled out of the room and down the endless turning of the staircase. The shadow was long and dark, now by my side, now leaping down the stairs before me, now rearing up the walls behind. The thing was horrible, insane. I burst out into the brightly lit central hallway and stumbled to a halt, backing up against the wall as I did so. There was nothing with me. A tram rattled past outside on its way up Dame Street. I stood there for a few moments gasping for breath. Somehow I was still clasping that loathsome book. I did not look at it. As soon as I was in any state to do so, I re-entered the Provost's drawing-room. It is scarcely necessary to say that its urbane Hanoverian splendour helped as much as anything to restore my self-control. Mrs Traill was serving tea. I handed the book to the Provost. I do not think he noticed my eagerness to be rid of it.

"With the compliments and apologies of Dr Stearne," I remarked with contrived facetiousness. "Please accept it freely as a gift."

The Provost received the book gravely. His very presence was almost sufficient to assure me that my imagination had merely run riot.

"Thank you," he said, "I am sure Dr Abbott, our librarian, will be glad to have it back. I will have it delivered to him in the morning. Where did you say it is marked?"

"On the first page of the text and again somewhere about page 46, I think."

The Provost was sitting to the left of the fire with his back to a window which opened onto the twilight of evergreens and mulberry trees beyond. The new electric light was low down and slightly forward of him so that his shadow spread up the wall by the window in a way which I did not like to see. He turned the pages carefully according to my directions and then looked up.

"I don't see anything here, Mr Ross. Perhaps I have the wrong place?"

I walked reluctantly round to the back of his chair and looked over his shoulder without touching the book. He had it open at the right place. But the page was as crisp and clean as the printer's ink had left it. I stared incredulously. My eyes hungrily devoured the sentences seeking some trace of the alterations or underlining that I remembered, but there was nothing. I leaned forward, and in doing so placed my hand near the Provost's shoulder. "When you have shut your Doors, and darkened your Room, remember ..." In my eagerness and vexation I half murmured the words aloud. But a cry from the Provost's wife and a clatter of china interrupted me.

"Oh Mr Ross, come away, come away," she gasped.

"What *is* the matter?" The Provost's question was addressed to his wife, not to me, but I quickly returned to her side. I had some inkling of what she had seen. It had not been imagination.

"Your shadow ..." She hesitated. "Your shadow ... your hand ..."

"Oh come, come, my dear! It is nothing, just the position of the lamp. There, I'll remove it."

The Provost was at his strongest, most self-controlled, and his wife responded. But she remained pale and silent.

"Are you certain you saw the name and alterations?" the Provost asked when we were seated again.

It was on the tip of my tongue to say yes, emphatically yes. But something whispered caution to me. I had already seen too much. I did not want to know more.

"It is true that I was suffering from a megrim when I first examined it," I said. "But I did look again shortly afterwards. And another point which occurs to me – where would I have got the name Johannes Stearne if I had not seen it in the book? It was quite strange to me at the time."

"Yes, but I think you are wise to be cautious ... You see, this book was printed in 1759. Stearne – at least the last Stearne to be associated with this college – died in 1745. It is said that he was insane at the end. Be that as it may, there can be no possible connection between him and this book." I felt the reproof, but I also felt the chill of things beyond reason.

"We must look at his memorial tomorrow," he continued. "Meanwhile, perhaps I should not delay you further. You must be very tired after your long journey. Thank you for the Epictetus." He placed it on the corner of a long bookcase. It was evident that he had been perfectly unaware of anything unusual about the book or my behaviour. His wife was more perceptive. We were all standing up and saying good night when the Provost caught my elbow.

"It has just crossed my mind", he said, "that we can look at dear old John Stearne on the way upstairs. His portrait – well, at least a mezzotint – hangs on the stairs. You will have passed it already. We had better look at it tonight because it is being removed early in the morning. It is going to Yeats – you know, the father of W.B., our new Ireland poet – to be recreated in oils." I did not want to follow him, but had no alternative.

The Provost mounted the stairs in front of me and stopped by a dark, almost life-sized head-and-shoulders engraving. The head was turned slightly to the left. The eyebrows were straight and thick, the lower jaw and lip thrust forward, the mouth unused to laughter, the nose broad and pendulant, the eyes cold and staring. Wisps of black hair obscured the ears and forehead, and blended into a dark skullcap. But it was the background to the head which transfixed my attention. It was not an illusion. The engraver had drawn the folds in Stearne's gown in a most curious way at the left shoulder: a way which I had already seen. Apart from that I perceived a man unbeloved of the gods; old, ugly and haunted. A man for whom death would be a release from the brooding, watching fear which the engraver had somehow contrived to portray for those who could see. And there was more. I knew that it was familiar to me; that something from the deathless night of the soul which had afflicted Stearne had drawn near and been my companion. I turned away and followed the Provost up the long winding stone staircase. I should have felt afraid but I was not. There was no sense of a dark companion now I had given the book away and it had been freely accepted. The picture was nothing fearful in itself, and it had been removed before I came down the next morning. I never saw it again. But I have sometimes wondered what this Yeats made of it.

At breakfast the Provost mentioned that his wife had already instructed a skip to take the Epictetus across to Abbott's rooms. I didn't meet Abbott or hear from him until my last few days in Dublin when I received a letter. He had been taken ill on the morning after my arrival and was sorry not to have met me. He thanked me for "the peculiar volume". His letter continued: "The Provost mentioned that you had connected it with Stearne and in a peculiar way this may be so. I have been able to confirm its date of first entry in the Library records, and its subsequent loan to one Hamilton who was instructed by the board to construct a memorial for Stearne. Unfortunately there was an estrangement shortly after the completion of his task between Hamilton and the Provost and nothing more was heard of the book until you so kindly returned it. I expect you have already seen the memorial."

I had not. The Provost had forgotten his suggestion to show it to me. But I made it my business to see it for myself. I found it just before my departure from the college. It was in a damp, cheerless little corner to the north-east of the chapel, heavily shadowed by the proximity of the dining-hall. To the left of the memorial to a Dr Steele, and above the macabre crystalline ruins of the effigy of Luke Challoner, the college's first provost, was a decomposing tablet recording Stearne's life and work. It was unremarkable except for one item. The epitaph was headed, not with a scriptural text as is proper, but with a sentence from Epictetus: ΚΑΤΑΡΑ ΕΣΤΙ ΜΗ ΑΠΟΘΑΝΕΙΝ. Which is to say: "It is an accursed thing not to die." I resisted the temptation to dwell upon what unpleasant aptness the text might have for Stearne. It is sometimes an advantage to be constitutionally blind to superstition and professionally hostile to metaphysical theories. As I set out for the station I resolved to record the matter as accurately as I could, and thereafter to resist speculation. I have kept both resolves.

My grandfather's narrative ends there. I have tried to check what he says but it is as if time has deliberately confounded the evidence. The memorial as seen by my grandfather was described by Burke in 1891, but now there is no trace of it: just a blank wall. The mezzotint has disappeared, and J.B. Yeats' copy of the portrait, while certainly showing a man of unusual ugliness and almost simian features, does not have a background which suggests anything to me. But it is hung in a gloomy position and is difficult to see clearly. I have of course looked for the Carter Epictetus in the college library but without success. Perhaps significantly, the Librarian's Board Report for 1856 remarks that "only one volume was found to be missing" (and that among so many thousand!). The 1872 printed catalogue contains no mention of it, as one would expect if it had been removed in the eighteenth century, and not returned until my grandfather's visit. The guard books which list additions between 1872 and 1963 ought to be more helpful but are not. Much more recently a new and fine copy has been acquired by the Doneraile Collection, but the volume has a history quite different from the one my grandfather found. It is entirely possible that Abbott failed to return it to the library since he never recovered from the illness which my grandfather mentions and died within six months. Possibly having been returned it was inaccurately catalogued or inadvertently placed on a shelf without being listed at all. I am not like my Victorian grandfather – learned, devout and sceptical in one self-regulating mix. I have often browsed in the dusky vastness of the Long Room, in the days when fellows of the college took precedence over tourists, and wondered if the corrupt Epictetus is there somewhere, lost among the memorials of the many generations that guard that awesome place. I see it now: the remote oaken vault of the great ceiling, the centuries of books receding bay by bay, gallery upon gallery, into the distant focus of a doorway where there are always shadows.

I should perhaps add that my grandfather returned safely to Aberdeen and never wrote about the matter again in his journals; nor, apparently, did he suffer from the "depression and uneasiness" which afflicted him while the uncommon memorial to Dr Stearne was in his possession.

Avernus

I see it now: thin fingers of an elm
Against the sky;
The waiting silence of a setting sun,
The frozen fields;
And in the west a tracery of red
Drawn out across the hills.
And then the dark and swift embrace of snow.

Times Gone

A t the foot of a sombre expanse of moorland in one of the more northerly counties of England there is a small, old, inconspicuous cottage. You may have walked thoughtlessly past it on a summer day or looked at it from the tourist road across the valley without ever realizing it was there. But even if you had seen the cottage, it is unlikely that the soft stone walls, the mossed roses, and dark windows would bring to mind anything of the fear of ancient things which once seemed to reach down towards it from the hills. It is equally certain that no such fear was in the

minds of either of the two young men who made their first, hesitating way towards it in the early twilight of a December day in
the year – but perhaps I should not tell you the year. To the young
it will seem long ago; to the old a time more real than the present,
and to me – why to me it is a dream forgotten: something shriv-
elled and gone.

The two students, for such they were (let us simply call them
Mark and Edward), were from opposite ends of the mongrel
inheritance which is England. Edward was tall and fair, his limbs
well-proportioned and athletic, his character as open as a Sussex
landscape. His father was a bus driver. The other man, Mark, was
lightly built, with black hair and almost Italianate skin and features. His manner was restrained. His deep brown eyes suggested
hidden thoughts and suppressed feelings. His father was a highly
successful barrister. It may be that he envied the confidence and
strength of his companion. Be that as it may, each liked the other
in that immediate, easy, enthusiastic way which marks early
friendships. That was how it began.

It seemed a brilliant idea when they first discussed it at tea one
afternoon after returning from the river (Mark was cox for their
college's first VIII, Edward its stroke). What about a reading holiday before Schools – that most dreaded and most rewarding of
final examinations? Each would help keep the other to his task
without allowing the solitary brooding which so often led to disaster. And chance had so readily assisted the enterprise. Mark had
not been looking for the advertisement. It just caught his eye: a
furnished cottage for short winter let. He did not know – he could
not possibly have foreseen – that this was the first step on the way
to an event that would cast its shadow forward into their lives'
end. But it all began urbanely: on the unfashionable side of
Oxford Station at the end of term, on a day when rain and smoke

and the smell of gas seeped into the wet stones and mingled with steam and engine smoke along the platforms. And now, in a colder and cleaner air, they were near to their destination. They walked along the valley, chatting occasionally, but for the most part tired and silent after the long journey. The way took them down an empty lane, over the river by the white footbridge, and then along muddy fields to the first rising of the ground above the floor of the valley. The cottage itself was up a steep lane. About a hundred yards before reaching it they found Mrs Fenwick's cottage where it had been arranged for them to collect the keys. She was the nearest and only neighbour – kind but garrulous – and by the time they were allowed to go on again (refreshed by tea) it was quite dark.

The cottage was unusual. There was a single, large living-room into which the outside door opened directly, a small bedroom, a tiny kitchen, and a minute bathroom, all opening off the big room. But it was the furniture that was so striking. It was heavy oak, black with age. An immense four-poster bed, richly over-wrought with Jacobean carving on head and canopy, filled one corner of the living-room. The windows of the place were small. The fireplace contained an iron range, with an open fire on one side of it. It was set into an inglenook of great stone beams which someone had painted a sombre red. The atmosphere was cold and still. But the kitchen and bathroom had recently been added to the original building. Both were simple and economical; both were well equipped. There was electric light and running water, and Mrs Fenwick had been in to set the fire. Within a few minutes she was in again with a store of newly aired blankets and linen. The atmosphere thawed. The fire burnt with clear young flames. The dust of arrival settled. The beds were made and their books set out on the Welsh dresser which occupied half of one wall. As

Edward observed, "Things could be a lot worse." Not long after supper he disappeared to sleep in the small room. He was the sort of man who would always prefer cold rooms and spartan exercise to comfort and electric blankets. Mark climbed thankfully into the four-poster. The last he remembered was firelight, and the sense of warm sleep stealing over him. But as he fell asleep he also seemed to hear, far away, the baying of hounds, and his dreams were of dark rivers and ruins.

In the morning Mark woke first. The door of the cottage was at the back. When he opened it – they had arrived in the dark – he found himself looking up through a lattice of bare ash trees at the black ridges of hills which rose directly to the south, dominating and darkening the skyline. In the other direction he could see across the valley to the village of Thorpcot, and on beyond it to brilliant banks of light in the distance which were the snow-covered Cheviots. Later that day, when they were shopping in the village, he asked about the southern hills. The first high ridges, he was told, were Wittonfell. Beyond them lay the great empty expanses of Fallowlees Moor. At one time a few poor farms had been worked, but wind and heath had long since made them unfindable, and now only the mapmaker or occasional shepherd visited the moor. Mark said nothing, but the love of desolate places and silent dwellings was already in his soul, and he was drawn to it like a salmon to the sea.

During the first few days at the cottage, while the weather became steadily colder, both men settled into a routine of study broken only by shopping for provisions, cooking, and short, brisk walks along the river, always, it seemed, in the shadow of Wittonfell. It was about a week after their arrival that Mark – again inadvertently – stumbled upon the information which gave him the excuse he sought. He had been reading for a couple of hours after supper, searching Hesiod for traces of a source for Virgil's account of capturing a swarm of bees, when he suddenly flung down the volume in disgust and disappeared into Edward's bedroom to seek diversion in the small collection of books they had found there. In a moment he was back with a faded publication. Edward did not look up from his mathematical pursuits.

"May I interrupt you?" Mark inquired at length.

Edward still did not move. Mark regretted speaking.

"I think you have. What is it?"

"Something interesting here. It's not long."

Edward raised an eyebrow questioningly.

"It's a guide book to this area, printed in 1908."

"What about it?"

"An account of Thorpcot – splendidly formal – listen." He extended his feet comfortably towards the fire and read.

Thorpcot has been somewhat generally recognized as a health resort for upwards of fifty years, but as a rural retreat, a place where the mind may be purified and the body rebuilt, the wonder and charm of a wild countrywide be felt and enjoyed, it has been known for a much longer time. One of the principal attractions for the visitor will be a walk to Wittonfell. The ground is often very wet near to the highest levels, and there are some swampy patches on Fallowlees Moor near Loch Abern into which the unwary traveller can be engulfed if care is not taken to select the dry and firm ground but, in the Author's opinion, the lofty elevation provides one of the finest walks to be taken in any part of England. There is a fine preserve of grouse near to the summit kept by Lord Alnworth, and on the far side from Thorpcot there are several considerable earthworks which most authorities consider to be Roman field camps, although Dr Tomlinson attributes them to a much earlier period.

Mark looked up. "What about a walk up there tomorrow if the weather holds? We've been rather good about work, and I fancy looking at the earthworks. You might like the exercise." He could not put his finger on the reason, but he felt as if he were asking for a favour. Perhaps it was because he very much wanted to go, but was reluctant to go alone.

"Yes, I probably would." Edward hesitated. "Does it say anything else of interest?"

"I don't think so. Wait a minute. There's another paragraph ... just a story."

In recent years the central area of Fallowlees has been little inhabited, although in living memory one of the crofts was held by a remarkable local character. The man was employed as a shepherd but such was his lonely industry that he mastered the intricacies of several classical languages and became something of an authority on the relics of ancient civilizations on Fallowless. It is sad to relate that his undisciplined studies led him to wild, and it is to be feared superstitious speculations about the nature of some of these relics. The Author has been unable to discover the fate of this rustic scholar, but it is probable that he sought employment elsewhere.

"That's all there is of interest," he said. "The next section is about Cartington. Let's go and have a look in the morning. We've got boots."

Edward smiled wryly. "All right," he said. "We've been pretty good about work, and I don't suppose it will make any difference in the long run."

"I wonder ..." Mark mused to himself. But he was wondering about the rustic scholar, not about the long run of things concerning which we all prophecy with such careless ease.

It was about ten o'clock when the two men began to make their way up the frosty slopes of Wittonfell. On the top they turned south-east towards Blueburn and then, about midday, swung round west in order to cross the central area of Fallowlees. Mile after mile of undulating heather and bog grass, occasional outcrops of grey sandstone, brown patches of marsh and dead bracken rolled away into the horizon. The whole was curiously unconfined, and its edges were a grey twilight that could have been sky or hill.

It was two o'clock when they came to the roofless walls of a cottage situated in the middle of a system of low banks and ditches which could possibly have been of military origin. Mark said as much. But the country was more or less between Dere Street and the Devil's Causeway – the old supply lines to the Antonine Wall – and he had no recollection of anything being found in that area. The ruin could have been the home of the scholarly shepherd. But there was nothing to indicate whether it was or was not.

Two hundred yards or so beyond the cottage, a defile of considerable depth opened up to the north through one of the undulations of the moor.

"What about having lunch here?" Edward suggested.

Mark had no reason he could voice for not doing so, except that the place was shadowy and cold. It was also quiet. So quiet that as they sat eating bread and cheese and drinking coffee from a thermos they both lowered their voices. Mark caught himself listening for some background noise which would give dimension to the place. From the silence and their muffled conversation they might have been sitting in an overgrown cave. He felt closed in and suffocated. Then, as he watched, he experienced that peculiar resetting of the mind which is recognition. He knew the place, He had sat there before. But of course he couldn't have been there before. He had never been that far north. But the feeling was disconcerting, and it grew stronger.

He stood up as soon as he decently could.

"We'd better go. It's getting late," he said.

"Yes, and cold." Edward scrambled to his feet. "I think that's our way," he pointed north through the corrie.

The corrie – perhaps glen is a better word – was about twenty yards wide, and at most a hundred feet deep. It ran through the hill in a north-south direction, its sides overgrown with long heather. A wide shingly path, or possibly it was an old water course, found a way along the bottom. In some places it was blown over with a little fine snow. But Mark was not observing the path minutely. It was as if he was walking into a future he had already seen. Without precisely knowing what he would see next, the way was familiar, and he had the overwhelming sense that it led to some unpleasant end that he could not avoid. He hung back, casting about for an excuse for delay, but nothing offered itself. Edward was a little way ahead.

"Wait a minute," Mark called. And then, as he caught up, "Do you sense anything odd about this place, or is it my imagination?"

"Not really. Except that it's cold and dark. Let's get on."

The twilight had drawn in on them suddenly. The sun was already far set, and one side of the corrie was little more than shadow broken here and there by snow. Mark followed helplessly.

A little way ahead the enclosing banks opened out again onto the moor, but their path turned aside, as Mark anticipated, to pass round a small lake. It was one of several they had seen during the day. But unlike the others it was black, and still, and completely unfrozen in the prolonged mid-winter frost.

"That must be Loch Abern," Edward remarked carelessly, still hurrying on.

They were half-way round the lake when Edward dislodged something which rolled on ahead in the black peat and stopped. He scooped it up, glanced briefly at whatever it was, and slipped it into his pocket.

"Bit of metal. Coin of some sort," he said.

Mark had also stopped, but was paying little attention. He was looking at a grey miasma that was drifting down from the mouth of the corrie behind them. The thing seemed to have a malevolence of its own, a purpose and intention utterly different from the still autumnal mists in which he had seen cattle standing in fields at home. It drifted down and out over the lake behind them.

"For god's sake go on!" he snapped suddenly. "Go *on* Edward!"

"Sorry, I didn't mean to hold up the party. I was just listening. You did ask me if I noticed anything odd about the place. Well I do. There are no birds here. Nothing since we stopped for lunch. All right. I'm coming!" he added as Mark set off without a word at a pace which he did not explain. Behind them the mist advanced to the edge of the lake, and crept over the path.

Earlier in the day the whole moor had been clear and bright in winter sunshine. But at evening the sun came as an almost horizontal light. Every depression was filled with a pool of darkness, and they laboured up a half-seen path towards a silhouette of hill. It was in a way very beautiful, but also sharp and unnatural, and Mark, still ill at ease, caught himself watching his own shadow – a giant form that walked to his right. Somewhere behind them a grouse chuckled in the heather. It was an ordinary, common sound, and welcome after the silence of the lake. A moment later the bird flapped off with its usual "go back-go-back-go-back-back-back-back-back" and then flew straight at them, winging low over the ground. At the last moment it gave another startled exclamation and changed course to fly away at right angles. They both stopped.

"That's the first grouse I've seen," remarked Edward.

"It was a very curious one."

"Why?"

"Grouse will not fly towards you unless they are put up by beaters or startled in some way."

"That one did."

They both looked back at the darkening expanse of moor. Freezing fog was already covering the path they had taken, and was visibly gathering in the folds of hills. Mark could find nothing to say, and they walked on silently.

As they crossed the top of Wittonfell and began to descend, the altered lie of the land brought the edge of the sun up off the horizon again. In the distance an unbroken line of long white hills marked the bounds of Scotland. Below, the heather slopes swept down to the farmlands. Across the river Mark could see Thorpcot, trails of smoke rising straight up from its chimneys; a grey, ageless village surrounded by strips and squares of fields. The trees were sharp and hard in the winter light. The setting sun beamed into his eyes from its rest on the hill above Holystone. The whole harmonized man and winter like a Flemish painting. And yet something alien had walked with him on the hills, and it was with him still. Mark desperately wanted to speak, but could find no words to begin. Edward would not understand.

They walked on down the last slopes to the cottage. The sun set red and cold. The sheep stood still, huddled together in the fields, their breath hanging in clouds over them. No living thing moved in all the landscape.

In a few minutes they were home. Mark busied himself with supper. Edward lit the fire. By the time they were eating, the living-room was warm and cheerful. The copper pans on the dresser glinted in the fire light. The rows of willow pattern and pewter plates looked down with mellow faces. The cottage relaxed contentedly around them. Outside, a December twilight gave way to the darkness of stars upon which no moon intruded.

When they had finished and the things were cleared away, Edward opened his books at the table. Mark retreated to the fire with a copy of the *Orestia*. At first he read quickly, but soon his eye began to wander more and more slowly along the line of print, and his attention left the page. He caught himself listening for sounds in the cottage or outside it. With an effort he worked over the page again. Again his eyes followed the words while his thoughts wandered back to the mist blowing over the lake. Again he reached the bottom of the page without knowing in the least what it was about. At the third attempt the book slid onto the floor and he jerked up with a guilty start.

"I'm nearly asleep too after that long walk," said Edward sympathetically, but not quite understanding. He closed his books. "What were you dreaming about?"

"I was thinking about the corrie. It's a queer place. I felt ... if those were earthworks at its south end I think they must be pre-Roman. That reminds me – what was it you found?"

"I'll get it," said Edward rising from the table. "Where did you put it?"

"I didn't put it anywhere. I presume it's still in your pocket."

Edward walked over to where the coats were hanging on the door. A wind had risen and was gusting and buffeting round the little croft. The coat swung gently to and fro in a draught. For a moment Edward hesitated. Then he hurried back to the fire.

"What's the matter?"

"Nothing," he replied. "It's not very light by the door and after having had my head in that book for an hour in bright light I couldn't see for a moment. It's all right. Don't fuss," he added as Mark continued to look at him. "Tell me about this thing." He tossed it over.

It was a coin-like disc, about two inches across, probably made of bronze. On one side a tree with creatures intertwined in the branches was just discernible under the dirt. On the other, a complicated and much clearer picture depicted some form of sacrifice. On the left was a tripod and fire with a priestess standing beside it with a cup in her hand. In the centre were four bullocks in a row looking towards her while behind them on the right cowered a group of men, some of whom appeared to have staves or swords in their hands. The background was filled with something too vague and worn to be interpreted: it could have been woods or rocks or other dark figures. The edges of the disc were rough and unmilled.

As Mark examined it, at first carelessly and then with rising excitement, he was conscious of a whole sequence of emotions – interest, the relish of discovery, surprise, awe at the age of the thing, and finally the chill of recognition. It was not merely *some* pagan ritual, but a specific picture which would not quite come out of his memory but which disturbed him in some direct way as he had been disturbed – no frightened was the truth – up by Loch Abern. It was somehow the *same thing* in another form.

"What is it?" Edward's question cut into his reverie.

"It's not a coin," he said. "I'm nearly certain it's genuine. It's a fantastic thing to have found. It's late Roman, maybe third or fourth century AD. Look at the way the figures are overclothed and losing their classical realism. But the sacrifice is normal pagan ritual as far as I can tell. There's nothing Mithraic or Christian there."

"Yes, but *what is it?*"

Mark hesitated. His experience of antiquities was not wide enough to be sure, but he could guess. "I think it's some sort of amulet. Have a look. Be careful."

"Is it valuable?"

"I don't know. But it's precious."

Edward turned it over in his hand. "Is it safe to wash the thing?" he asked.

"Oh yes. But just use soap and running water. Don't pick at it with anything sharp."

Edward disappeared into the bathroom. In a few moments he was back.

"Have another look," he said.

The effect of washing was to show up some small letters scratched into the metal of the unmilled edge. One word was in each quadrant.

"This is not part of the original," said Mark. "Someone's done this comparatively recently."

"What does it mean?"

"INICE – TU – MIHI – TERRAM. No, better: TU MIHI TERRAM INICE – Cast earth on me."

Mark stared unseeingly into the fire.

"*Tu mihi terram inice* ... I know that phrase ... It's somewhere in Virgil ... Virgil ... That's it! Of course!" He almost leapt out of the chair as he spoke.

"Of course what?" Edward looked at him in surprise. Mark was not easily excited.

"'*Spelunca alta fuit, vastoque immanis hiatu.*' It's all right. I'll explain," he added quickly. "This afternoon up by the lake, you must have noticed how preoccupied I was."

"Yes I did. I thought you were put out about something."

"No, no, not at all. It was just that I had the strangest sense of having been there before – you know the feeling – and the place, I don't know, it somehow oppressed me. Now I know why. I'd seen it in reading Virgil. '*Spelunca alta fuit*, a deep cave there was, opening wide and vast, shingly and sheltered by dark lake and gloom, over which no birds could wing their way, whence it is that the Greeks spoke of Avernus, the Birdless Place.' That's it! I may have got it slightly wrong, but that's the gist of it. Can't you see it? Virgil's description of the entrance to Hades, the land of shadows and the dead?"

"Yes," Edward grinned. "I think I do see how it could have struck you. Even I noticed the lack of birds. May I look at the amulet again?"

Mark handed it to him. Edward turned it over several times in his hand looking rather preoccupied.

"What is it?"

"Nothing. Nothing really." He placed it carefully on the table. "I'm rather chilly," he said. "I'll get some cocoa before we go to bed."

When he returned, Mark was curled up quietly on the sofa reading. It had been the most enormous relief to identify the pre-cognition which had so troubled him on the moor, and which had again tugged at him through the medium of the amulet. The sense of disquiet and apprehension had simply been the result of a sub-consciously recognized similarity between where they had been and the vast, shadowy picture previously implanted in his mind by the divine poet. The rest had been the embellishments of his imagination. But the mist had been real enough, and so was the amulet. Evidently someone else a long time ago, and again more recently, had associated the place with Virgil's sombre description of the entrance to Hades. Possibly the amulet had been brought there and lost by – or with – one of the legionaries who for three centuries helped to protect Roman order from the barbarians at the ends of the world. Possibly the learned shepherd had found it. At that point the glass darkened again. The shepherd had gone, and the memory of him had all but vanished. Then the thing had declared itself once again for Edward to find.

"Drink up! It'll get cold." Edward was standing with his back to the fire. Mark returned from far away with a start.

"Oh, thanks. Yes it's fascinating."

Edward eyed him with tolerant disapproval. "Don't work too late. I'm going to bed," was all he said.

"I'm going myself in a minute."

But he remained seated while Edward pottered about. At length he got up and went over to the door to look out, as he usually did last thing. It was extraordinarily dark. The wind which had been blowing earlier had subsided leaving an almost oppressive silence. A coal slipped in the grate behind him. A rafter gave a slight tick. Somewhere out in the freezing fog a dog was barking. The heavy vapour swirled in at the open door like smoke. The cold was intense.

He closed the door carefully and tidied up the books, once more uncertain of himself and of his thoughts. *Spelunca alta fuit ...* the words chased round in his brain like the beat of unwanted music. Edward was still doing something in the kitchen. If only he would stay, reading late into the night as they so often did. But even as the hope came to him, his companion looked in, said goodnight, and disappeared into the adjacent room firmly closing the door.

Mark undressed slowly. The cottage was very quiet and it was hard to avoid a temptation to move about stealthily. He heard Edward settle down to sleep in the little bedroom. His friend could switch consciousness on and off like an electric light, and Mark envied him. A few minutes later he too turned out the lights, and climbed into the great antique bed that filled one corner of the living-room. He lay still, watching until his eyes became accustomed to the darkness. The embers in the grate cast a dull red glow by which it was just possible to distinguish the familiar features of the room, except for an area of shadow near the door. He turned over onto his back and stared up at the black canopy of the bed. The carved figures stared down at him with invisible eyes. The shadows in the room darkened.

There followed an indefinite period of time during which the fire sank to a dull red spot and the darkness by the door extended to fill the whole room. Mark thought he slept. At least he was conscious of turning over, and then of a period of oblivion before a half vision of the room came back to him, and then faded into a void through which he moved lucklessly and against his will. A moon came up upon his left, and then he was in a dark woodland, silent and empty. A bitter wind plucked and tore at him. He could see the wind like a living thing, and he knew it was cold, but there was neither sound nor feeling to it, only a remote fear. He was alone in a great space of land. It was night, but he knew the scene already. At the far end was the entrance to a cleft in the rock: somewhere before him a dark lake. He was waiting for something to come out of the rock towards him. He struggled to turn away, but the scene moved with him. And then he knew that two figures were making a way out of the cavern towards the lake. He tried again to avert his eyes but the thing had him in thrall. The leading figure was walking down towards the water where a fire had been prepared beside a tripod, and the figure was walking upright as a man should, but it was a very old man. Behind him a tall youth was leading a ram with a halter about its neck. But it was the youth who was oiled and decked with flowers.

Then another movement caught Mark's attention, something dark and shadowy flitting and flowing down from the cavern, something which filled him with fear and made him want to cry a warning; but the men by the lake continued to work with their backs to the cavern, unaware of the dreadful thing they were bringing upon themselves. The old man held something round and glistening towards the fire, beckoning as he did so to his attendant. Then the shadow fell on them both. Mark saw the old man's hand flung up in the sign to repel evil. For a moment the face of the youth was turned so that Mark could see him, then it was gone as darkness enveloped them both like the shadow of an eclipse racing across the earth. With all his will he urged himself back and away from the sacrifice, but he was no longer a separable part of what was happening. Fountains of flame surrounded him, scarlet branches waving in the wind, scourging him to the bone. He choked. He cried out. He fell helplessly forward into the silent fires which did not burn. As he fell, his eyes were open again.

He was aware of the bed under him. He was pressed down hard on it and was wide awake; yet some horror from the dream still lingered with him. He could see and feel and touch. His senses were clear and vivid. And he knew he was awake from the touch of the sheets and the beating of his heart. But he was unable to move. And he was not alone in the room. Something prevented him seeing the fire. The room was dark like a moonless night, dark like a cave, dark with the thing groping and flowing down to the water. Some evil force into which he was losing his soul moved over him. He forgot to breathe. His heart bounded and rushed. The mists rose up round him, feeling their way over the bed. A cry of abject terror burst out of him. The cold closed, pressed him down, down, suffocating and cold; down into the freezing fire at the heart of the universe.

"Mark! Mark!" He was being shaken.

With a gasp he fought up out of the depth, clutching at the familiar voice. The lights were on.

"Steady, steady. What's the matter?"

"I can't move ... The fire! I can't see!"

"The fire's out. Calm down!" Edward's voice was firm, but his hand was shaking. "It's six o'clock in the morning!"

Mark struggled to regain control of himself, but it was all too near.

"Don't go!" was all he could say, and then, "For god's sake, what was it?"

"Nothing as far as I can see. Something woke me, and then I heard you choking. It sounded a bit odd. I thought you were ill, so I came through."

"Thank heaven you came. Are you all right?"

"Of course I am. It was you I was worried about."

"It was dreadful."

"But what was the matter with you?" Edward was not looking at him as he asked the question, but out into the room .

"I don't know. A nightmare I think but that wasn't all. There was something moving in the room, and it was here when you woke me."

"There was nothing to be seen when I came in." Edward's voice was quite firm. It would have required a very alert observer to notice the hesitation. "And there's nothing here now. Do you want anything before I go back to bed?"

"No, I'm getting up. I've had enough of sleep for one night."

Mark was up as Edward began to protest, but he took no notice. He was half dressed before he saw the amulet. It was lying on the floor beside his bed. Edward was in his room putting clothes on with a great show of reluctance and resignation.

"Come and look at this."

"I expect you brushed it off the table when you were getting undressed last night." Edward picked up the amulet as he spoke, and replaced it quickly on the table.

Mark looked at him curiously, and then turned away without a word. The fire needed to be reset. By the time it was ready, Edward was making breakfast, but with surprisingly little resistance considering the hour. Neither of them said anything until they had eaten.

"Look here," Mark began at length. "I know you must think I'm mad and had a nightmare, and I did have a nightmare – about the first I've ever had in my life – apart from after drinking too much port at a meeting of the Taverners. But it wasn't just that. Some of it was real. There was something in the room when I woke. Didn't you see it? But never mind that now." He stopped awkwardly.

"Go on, you've got something else to say."

"That ruined cottage we saw up above the corrie yesterday – you remember – well do you remember the guidebook – the shepherd with his 'superstitious speculations'? And the cleft in the hill, and the lake, and the shingly path – you know what it all looked like – I told you last night. If the shepherd had read Virgil living there alone he couldn't have missed the similarity – the entrance to the underworld. Perhaps he found the amulet in the ruins and it set him thinking. Perhaps he scratched the inscription round its edge before it all went wrong. Perhaps he found something else, or ..." – Mark hesitated for a moment – "perhaps something found him."

The other man was looking blandly at him with those large blue eyes which never hid anything.

"For god's sake Edward! I'm afraid of that place! Can't you understand? Don't you know? But we must be rid of *that*." He pointed to where the amulet still lay. "Will you come up to the corrie with me and return it?" He hesitated, suddenly aware again that what he was saying made him seem weak and foolish. "I know

I'm mad, but the thing is *evil*. It's been misused in some way. I can't explain."

"Yes, I'll come," Edward agreed quietly. He picked up the amulet and drew breath to speak, then evidently thought better of it.

"Will you come now?"

"Yes, if it's clear, I mean if the mist's gone."

"Thank you."

It was still dark but entirely clear when they set off. Some of the stars were paling. The air felt remarkably free and empty. It was very cold. Somewhere a cock crowed, and the wind blew softly from the east.

By the time they were over Wittonfell it was full dawn, the light beginning to reveal the wonders worked by hoarfrost in the night. Half an hour later, as they approached the lake, it was daylight. Mark stopped. The morning sun had still not risen high enough to lighten the waters, and the place was full of shadows.

Edward handed him the amulet. "What do you want to do with it?"

Mark took it but didn't reply. He looked out over the water. What a small thing it was: only about thirty yards across and twice as long: really there was very little similarity to Lake Avernus. But in all the frost it was still unfrozen, and there were no birds. With a final look at the amulet he threw it into the middle of the pool. (I am now inclined to think this was a mistake. It was Edward's find. He should have retained it.) It disappeared without splash or sound.

"Did you expect a hand to appear and grasp it like Excalibur?" Edward's voice mocked his observance.

"I don't think I really expected anything to happen. The gods of the underworld weren't devils or demons. It was a place of emptiness and shadows and sleep: as death ought to be. The gods made death, men made the demons. And I fear the shepherd may have made more for himself than most men do."

He stood silently for a moment and then suddenly, as an after-thought, gathered up three handfuls of loose stones and earth and threw them, one after the other, over the surface of the lake. "*Tibi terram inicio*," he murmured almost inaudibly. As he spoke, the rim of the sun rose over the eastern flank of the hills.

And that should be the end of my story. But some stories never really end. They go on rippling down the lives of those they concern until, perhaps, we are all brought to the place where stories end. Mark and Edward lived out the rest of their stay at the cottage uneventfully, and returned to Oxford. In due course they got their degrees, and then drifted apart according to the way of the world. But never again were they as easy with one another as they had been before the events I have described: the one because he had said too much: the other because he had said too little. Mark because he had been too honest, and had almost laid bare some of the raw corners of his soul. Edward because he had not been able to bring himself to be honest enough. He had not explained that he had returned to the living-room in the night while Mark slept – and returned with the intention of using the amulet to play a mild practical joke upon his superstitious friend. But in the darkness he had knocked it off the table and been unable to find it. So he returned to bed with his joke incomplete. But more than that disturbed his memories. When he came back to the room on hearing Mark cry out, he had shone a torch over the bed before switching the light on. But the torch had shown him nothing but an opaque fog where the bed should have been: as if he were looking out beyond the walls of the cottage into the night. The effect had gone when he put on the main light. And as the years passed he remembered other things more and more vividly: the silence at the lake, the flight of the wild bird, the long shadows, and the darkness.

I know all this now because it so troubled him, silly fellow, that he wrote me a letter which was found attached to his will. As I read it, I realized how fortunate it was that I had not fuelled superstition by relating to him all the details of the nightmare, caused, as it undoubtedly was, by my overwork and worry about Schools. He said when his time came he would remember what I had said about death when I threw the amulet into the water. I have always regretted that amulet. The thing was priceless. But as I was saying, I have to confess that even I – tired, cynical, old man that I have become – even I felt some pale return of youthful awe about the destiny of things when I learnt from his widow how Edward died. I should not have been surprised: two hundred others died with him. I had already read unthinkingly about it in the newspapers. He was killed, along with all the other passengers, when his plane came down, in southern Italy, in Lake Avernus. I would once have cared so very much, but now, may the gods forgive me, the order of our going seems a very little matter. But it is curious all the same that his was the face of the unwitting victim turned towards me so long ago in the dream. EDWARDE, TIBI TERRAM INICIO.

Look Closely

Again, we do not say that one reality is the opposite of another. How then can a reality be constituted by things which are not realities? And how can that which is not a reality be prior to that which is?

Aristotle, *Physics*

Peter Manser was tired. It was the first time he had seriously prospected the garden. He had poked at the overgrown lawns, pushed past riotous hedges, and fallen into a partly concealed ditch. He had attacked roses that overflowed the crumbling brick paths. They had fought back with inward curving thorns from which it was almost impossible to break free without loss of blood.

It would take a lot of money, he decided, and time. Both had been unexpectedly thrust upon him by the blossoming of a long-held and largely forgotten premium bond, just as his own long-held and largely forgotten position in Allied Chemicals was expunged with an EPNS handshake and an office party. An old house, a very old house, and a neglected garden set in the oak groves of a little valley on the western edge of Shropshire were the compensations chosen for him by his wife. He had not felt strong enough to demur.

But after two difficult winter months getting most of the house sorted out, the prospect of the garden remained discouraging. It wouldn't be so bad when old Neville kept his promise and came regularly to help, but now, left to himself, Manser didn't know where to begin, and at the precise moment when he was tired and wishing he could be back in the ordered semi-detachment of the familiar plot in Solihull, he had come across an ugly inscription cut on an oblong of slate and framed by heavy stone slabs like a Victorian grave.

It was hidden behind a curtain of juniper and cotoneaster on a raised part of the boundary wall about a hundred yards from the back of the house. He could not translate what was written, but certain words suggested ideas which health care and a secure job had kept at a distance. He let the bushes spring into place again, and remained still for a time before suddenly, as if disturbed from a daydream, looking back at the house. He could see, and be seen, from every window. His wife was watching him now. He looked again and was on the point of waving at the laughing face when he realized it was nothing more than a mark on the old curtain that still hung at one of the ground-floor windows. It didn't even look like a face when he looked properly, let alone his wife's. What was, however, certain was that if he cleared the overgrown bushes shielding the boundary wall, the monument, or whatever it was, would be seen every time someone did in fact look out of a window. The thing would have to go. If he and Monica were ever to make this place their own, these persistent reminders of whoever had been there before – and this was not the first he had come across – must go. It wasn't as if this one was particularly old. Maybe twenty or thirty years? There was no way of telling with slate and there was no date on it to help. Since there seemed to be no name either, it probably wasn't a memorial, but a translation would be interesting. Manser thought it was Latin, and the impression was strengthened as he pencilled the words on a scrap of paper. The end of the inscription, MORTUUS INIURIAM ACCIPIAM, was located low down at the right-hand corner. As he bent down to check the spelling, something carved on the wall below it caught his eye. He pulled away the tangle of old grass. A moss-encrusted face, perhaps meant to be smiling, but perhaps ...

"Peter dear, do give it up for today. You've done enough."

With a movement of quite startling speed Manser jerked upright and contrived to turn round at the same time.

"I'm sorry. Did I give you a fright?"

"I didn't hear you. I thought you were somewhere in the house."

"Sorry. What were you looking at?"

"Nothing much. Just the wall. There's a sort of inscription behind these bushes. You'll see it when I've cleared them. I was copying it out. Here it is if you want to look. You won't understand it," he added with more truth than tact.

Monica looked at the paper uncomprehendingly.

"Yes," she said, then "I came out to say lunch is ready."

He followed her back into the kitchen. Its large space of polished quarry tiles, pine tables and chairs, and the new Aga still charmed him every time he saw it – his house, *their* house. At least the house they intended to be their own, not the one forced upon them by an accident of employment and a speculative builder in the 1960s. Their intended house, but not, he sometimes sensed, a house wholly intended for him.

"Has Jimmy finished painting the dining-room yet?" he asked. "We'll need it tonight for Miss Hunter – and what's the man called?"

"William Blackstone. I wish you'd try to remember our neighbours' names. God knows there are few enough of them up here."

Manser shook his head. Monica had always looked after his social life. She was better with names than he was, and cared more about people. He had been content with his garden and an occasional holiday. She had always had wider horizons and sharper sympathies.

"Never mind that now," he said a little irritably. "Has Jimmy finished I asked."

"I know you asked. I was just going to tell you. I've been very busy while you've been pottering outside. He's helped of course. I expect he'll charge us for the time – everyone does these days – but it was kind of him. He's done a lovely job painting, and we've got all the carpets and furniture in place. So it's finished. He left a few minutes ago. Don't look now. I'll get ready for our dinner party before you see it. Miss Hunter will be surprised tonight. When she called that first week, she said she hadn't been in the house for years. I'm sure she will be able to tell us lots about the place we don't know. She knows *everybody*. Don't you want any chocolate sponge?"

Manser smiled at her. His attention had been wandering. She still did things which charmed and surprised him after thirty years of marriage, and the rearing of their three children.

"Have you been thinking what you want the garden to look like?" he asked. "It's really a choice between restoration and a complete restart on a simpler plan. I think ..."

"Oh, but we agreed to a restart," his wife spoke hastily. "It's hopeless as it is, all overgrown and closed in. We'll never get the mess tamed again. Let's open it all out to a fine lawn like we used to have. It's what you suggested and now we've got a view up to the woods we may as well make the most of it. That wall where you were working must go. Anyway it will be much less work for Neville, and he's not in his first youth."

Before Manser could reply that he wasn't either, his wife was asking what he intended doing that afternoon, and they were immersed in the amiable domestic to and fro of the actively retired. From this it emerged that Manser would drive the twenty or so miles to Ludlow for library books and shopping, while Monica would complete her preparations for the evening.

These took less time than she expected, and the idea came to her that she might have a preliminary look at the room at the back they had so far left alone – the room the house agent had described as the morning-room but which Peter had immediately said would be better called the evening-room since it faced west. They had agreed it would be for the TV, but had closed and locked the door so that it could be ignored while the rest of the house was being updated and decorated.

As soon as Monica went in she knew it would have been better left alone until someone could help her. Unfortunately she had been taught that you mustn't give up at the first difficulty; an unfortunate teaching because sometimes first difficulties are warnings of later impossibilities. So instead of retreating, she pressed on.

The big sash window was sealed with paint and dirt and no amount of effort could get it open to admit the spring air. The glass was semi-opaque with cobwebs. The remnants of net curtains still hung, stained with condensation. Dust, dead flies and whitish marks that could have been bird droppings covered the floor-boards. The grate overflowed with soot and twigs, and what

looked like a dead pigeon lay in a corner. At one side of the fireplace were a heap of old newspapers, unfathomable bits of dark
wood that might have come from a dresser or chimney-mantle
and, incongruously, a number of jam-jars. She looked apprehensively at the ceiling. That too would need work. The underside of
the floor-boards of their bedroom showed through between the
joists of ancient poplar where the lining paper had peeled away in
ugly curls. Worst of all, pictures and furniture that had once stood
against the walls had left grey outlines on the plaster, like profane
echoes of the Turin Shroud.

The whole house, she reflected, had been like this at first. But
not as bad. And it wasn't just the dirt. The villa in Anderson
Avenue had been hers. She had made it what it was among the
hundreds of others like it, just as Peter had created a garden that
was uniquely his out of a builder's plot. But Lentfield House carried the almost indelible marks of previous owners, like the nasty
little carvings she had found hidden on joists and inside cup-
boards; faces and worse that she had covertly smeared over with
polyfiller and new paint so that she wouldn't have to talk about
them with Peter. Only the kitchen felt really hers after they had
enlarged it out of the old domestic quarters. Everywhere else she
had to overcome a powerful aversion to altering anything. It was
even stronger than her reluctance to dismantle her father's little
house where he had lived since her childhood and on until the day
he died. Then it had been love, and sentiment, and memories that
made it so difficult. Now, and particularly in this room, it was her
feeling that she didn't belong, and that someone else did. Lentfield was not hers.

The fireplace was a mean, black little thing in cast iron, out of
proportion to the room, and out of character with the rest of the
house. Victorian she said to herself, not ... not ... well not whatever

seventeenth century was. The newspapers were copies of the *Daily Telegraph*, in date order of twelve years ago, but when she tried to open one it crumbled in her hand. The last was dated April 9th – tomorrow – but that one was still in the smooth elongated fold required to push it through a letter box. She put it back carefully, an uncomfortable thought forming in her mind, and turned again to the window. The sill was strewn with the desiccated bodies of wasps and fragments of flies. In one corner the faded wings of a vanished butterfly were held fast in the dust. When she tried to clean the glass behind the net, the cloth like funnels and drapes left by generations of spiders smeared to a grey haze through which she could dimly see silent birds darting about the garden. At her feet were the books, all bound in cloth that might once have been red but was now faded to a shabby fawn. She picked up the top one. Inside the cover was a book-plate, probably a woodcut thought Monica, who had once attended evening classes on illustration. It showed a long straight path through a formal garden partitioned by square-cut hedges. The path led to what looked like a tombstone, set in the centre of a low wall. Below it the artist had contrived to suggest a head or a face. Beyond the wall, trees and then hills receded into the distance. The artist had set the whole in a tracery of roses and brambles so fastidiously and minutely cut that the sides of the picture were lost in a whimsical haze of foliage. She raised her eyes, knowing that behind the uncut grass and overgrown foliage she would see the picture and the tomb Peter had uncovered that morning. What she was less prepared for was that she was standing at exactly the point from which the drawing had been made, the window frame cutting out the view precisely at the picture's edges. It was both interesting and vaguely disconcerting, and when she had finished comparing picture and subject she moved to the side before turning a page: Petronius, and then a name she had difficulty with, followed by another author, Seneca, and something utterly unpronounceable, APOCOLOCYNTOSIS. She laboriously followed the letters before opening the text at random, or rather not quite at random since a fold of paper had been used as a marker, and the book opened itself at that place. A short passage had been underlined in pencil and she couldn't avoid reading it. "A company acts a farce on the stage, one is called the father, one the son, and one is labelled the Rich Man. Soon the comic parts are shut up in a book, the men's real faces come back, and the made up disappear." Unconsciously her fingers came up to her own face and her imagination filled with the faces she had seen and hidden. This was awful. She dropped the book onto the floor and hurried back to the warm mediocrity of the kitchen, the paper marker still in her hand. On it she found several lines of writing, in pencil, in a strong italic script. As she read, she shuddered, and wished Peter home again. At the back of the house spiders began their silent restoration of the damage, while in her mind the words began their insidious work.

*

Miss Hunter lived in a charmingly old-world cottage about two miles down the valley from the Mansers. From her parlour she could sometimes see their lights against the darkness. She was small and thin and inclined to bird-like movements and soft woollen clothes. She had been born a very long time ago: so long ago that even she had contrived to forget exactly when it was. But she retained all the delight of a child in the possibility of doing new and exciting things, even to the extent of calling on new neighbours, or riding over strange paths in the hills on her gentle pony, or taking her shelty for walks at the top of the valley at summer sunrise (just because she knew life was *so* lovely). Her presence in the middle of the road in a tiny car as undatable as herself was a well-known local hazard. But to strangers the appearance of a vehicle driving itself could be alarming until thin fingers were discerned grasping the wheel from a position apparently somewhere below the dashboard.

On that particular evening William Blackstone, the other guest of the Mansers', had promised to pick her up on his way past. Her little car, she explained, didn't like the rough farm track up the hill, but she didn't think his Range Rover would mind. As they approached Lentfield, she wondered how the new arrivals were getting on. She felt they weren't quite at home up there away from their friends, but she was much too kind to say so, or even to think it in any clear way. It was a lovely evening, and Mrs Manser – she was already able to call her Monica – always did things in such a sweet and unusual manner.

By the time Miss Hunter had been shown into the drawing-room after powdering her nose, Blackstone, whose family she had known in the district for generations (although he himself always seemed to be abroad with colonial servants or whatever they had nowadays), was sipping sherry.

"Just a very small one please," she said. "My knees go all wibbly-wobbly if I have too much, but I *do* love Bristol Cream. Oh Monica, you *have* made a difference here. It's absolutely *delightful* and everything new! I would hardly recognize this room. It's so light. In the old days ..."

"We've done what we could," said Monica eagerly. "It was an uphill job, but very rewarding for Peter and I. Peter did most of the planning and Jimmy is a perfect gem as a house painter. He did up the hall and other rooms when we first came, but we only got

the dining-room finished this morning – sort of first showing."
She giggled nervously. "Sorry about the paint smell."

"He's a good tradesman," said Blackstone, rubbing back his
moustache. "One of the old school. Doesn't charge too much
either. Just as well I'm not his accountant."

"You knew the house in the old days Miss Hunter?" Manser
prompted gently.

"Oh *please* call me Dorothy. The other sounds so unfriendly.
Yes, I did in a way. It wasn't very nice really. Everything always in
a pickle. Little Miss Winter always used to say it was the sort of
house where you found dead insects on the window sills and last
week's cabbage under a cover somewhere. But I don't think he
could help it," she concluded vaguely. Monica was about to ask
who couldn't help it when Peter changed the subject.

"Would you and Mr Blackstone like to see what we've done
while Monica puts the finishing touches to the starter?"

The two guests dutifully followed their host while Monica
brought the prawn cocktails decorated with caviar into the dining-room on the far side of the hall.

It was not until after dinner, when the red tapered candles
were beginning to run into their cut-glass holders, and the
dimmed wall lights were reflecting pleasantly on the new
mahogany, that the conversation moved to the point which gave
Monica her opportunity. The progress to the point was casual, the
weather, the garden, the need for assistance, the question of
restoration or restart, and their preference for a restart.

"Excuse me," Monica said. "I found something quite interesting this afternoon that one of you might be able to tell us more
about, and Peter hasn't seen it yet. I'll not be a moment."

She returned with the book. It was only Manser who noticed
the slightly higher pitch to her voice and he forgot it afterwards.

"I found this in some rubbish this afternoon. You knew our predecessor Dorothy. Was that as he had the garden?" She knew the answer, and was unclear why she was asking, unless it was to gain some sort of reassurance, or just to talk about it.

Miss Hunter's frail but expressive face registered a querulous moue.

"Dear me. I don't think I want to look at this," she exclaimed in a wavering voice.

"But it's only an old book I found!"

"Well you see, I'm afraid, I don't want to say anything I shouldn't, but I didn't like his books and he sometimes wasn't a very nice man. It's only an opinion," she added hastily.

"Hardly knew him myself," remarked Blackstone. "He always seemed a scholarly little chap. Same college as me. But long before my time."

"He was horrid to dear little Ruby."

"Ruby?" Monica was at a loss, as she so often found herself with local people who seemed to know names and references without being taught.

"My shelty then."

"Ruby did have some slightly off-putting habits, you know," Blackstone smiled at her.

"Oh do you think so? He wore old lamb's-wool slippers and Ruby thought he was a sheep. He needn't have been so rude."

"I think he was just trying to make a joke out of it."

"You were going to tell us about the house," Manser reminded her.

"Was I? Oh yes. You see he used to sit on that bit of wall at the end of the garden – where he carved that silly inscription. He watched everything from there you know. And when he couldn't sit there any longer, because of his feet, he sat at the morning-room window, the room at the back you didn't show us, Peter. He used to sit there for hours and hours wrapped up in a shawl like an old spider." Miss Hunter looked very mournful. "He passed on, sitting there, in the night. Dr Chalk told me." She looked at the clock and then at the calendar on a desk across the room.

Manser had been peering over Miss Hunter's hand.

"How interesting," he exclaimed as he focused on the book-plate for the first time. "That's the garden as it must have been."

"Yes, that's his garden," continued Miss Hunter in a low voice. "He made it all. It was the one thing in the world he loved. He hated all the rest, the change and the disturbance. It must have been the last thing before – I remember posty telling me he brought a whole box of those stickers for his books. But he could-n't have had much time to stick them in. It was the day before –"

"I think this conversation is getting a bit sombre," Blackstone cut in. "He's gone long ago, and I think you are both making a splendid job of brightening the place up. It's a pleasure to see lights up here again. We thought it was going to be left to the four winds."

"Why was it empty for so long?" asked Manser, as his wife sug-gested they might move back to the lounge for coffee. "The ven-dor was someone in South Africa I heard. We only met the solicitor."

"I don't think he had any relatives," volunteered Miss Hunter, dabbing neatly at her mouth with a paper napkin before standing up. "They couldn't find the next of kin for ages, and it was held in Chancery or whatever happens when there's no will and nobody. But people came to look. They were always put off by something."

"Didn't they like it?" Monica asked. "We saw its potentials at once."

"I don't know. Someone said they couldn't face the challenge.

It's just a suggestion," she continued shyly, "But his garden was very unusual, very peaceful, and you might even get a grant or something to put it back."

Peter smiled. "No, Dorothy, we've quite made up our minds. It has to be cleared. We want an open view up to the woods and the setting sun."

"'Friends of flesh and bone are best: Comrade, look not to the west,'" murmured Blackstone, but no one noticed as Manser led them across the hall to the large room that had been the library.

In a few minutes Monica followed with coffee and liqueurs on a silver tray. Manser was speaking.

"Bill, I wonder if by any chance you might be able to help me with something. Someone said you had a classical education. It's the inscription I uncovered at the end of the garden today. You could see where it is from the book-plate. The sort of focus of the garden. I think it's Latin. I copied it out."

Blackstone looked doubtful. "I did read the Greats but it was a long time ago, and I'm very rusty. Let me see."

Manser had put the scrap of paper in his suit pocket earlier. As he handed it across, the other man slowly put on his spectacles, but whether from need, or to gain time, Manser could not tell.

"Let me see, yes, VALDE ENIM FALSUM EST ..., 'it is entirely false', that's to say wrong, 'for a man to cherish his house when alive and ...' ... something like 'not to care about where he must stay much longer'. CETERUM ERIT, MIHI CURAE ... 'I shall certainly take precautions ... in my will ...' NE MORTUUS INIURIAM ACCIPIAM ...' against injury being done to me when I'm dead.' That's roughly it. Vaguely portentous out of context. It's not Latin from the Golden Age. I'd say it was a quotation."

Manser was looking thoughtful. His wife sat very still, the coffee unpoured.

"I heard – I read that earlier today," she said. "It was on a piece of paper in the book I showed you. I felt –"

"That's what it is. Not classical Latin! A bit out of Petronius' foolery!" Blackstone positively bristled with satisfaction at the identification. "I beg your pardon Monica, I interrupted you."

"Oh no. It's quite al lright."

Manser cast a quick glance at his wife. She was frightened by something he thought, but before he could say anything Monica had added, "I was going to say I felt it was addressed to us."

"Nonsense!" exclaimed Blackstone.

"Oh no dear," said Miss Hunter in a concerned tone. "I expect it was just that he had to copy it out from somewhere for the mason. He was always very particular."

"Tell us about him," said Manser.

"No. I'd rather not tonight. It's a long story. Thank you, sugar please, then as soon as you've all had coffee I'd like to be going if Mr Blackstone wouldn't mind. It's been such a lovely evening."

"Would you care for something else?" asked Manser looking hopefully at Blackstone. "Port or whisky or something?"

The retired financial adviser to the Sultanate of al-Quattar did care for something else, and his house was too near and the law too remote for any contrary calculation to worry him. But as he ran Miss Hunter home a little later he was uncharacteristically silent.

"They're doing very well up there," he remarked suddenly, as if out of the end of an unspoken thought process. "Pity they buy their drawing-room furniture by the yard from Harrods. And that hall! Do you remember the wainscoting before they painted it?"

Miss Hunter said nothing, but her eyes twinkled in the dim light of the dashboard. As the car neared her gate she said, "I would never have dared to upset his arrangements. He was much too far sighted." Then she added, inconsequentially, "But Monica is very sweet."

Monica was washing up.

"We must get a dish-washer," she said and then, before Manser could agree or disagree, "I still think it would be best if we started again on the garden despite Dr Laris. Peter, I wish I hadn't seen that book with the picture in it or read that dreadful inscription. It's like someone telling us what we can and can't do. I feel watched, and when I look out of the back window I see it as he wanted it. Do you understand?"

Manser thought he did. He had already seen past the neglect to what had been, and could be again. But as he polished the plates he could find little to offer except a mumbled agreement, while in his mind's eye he drifted back to his own garden, the one *he* had made, and he was glad he did not know what had become of it any more than –

"We never got his name." Monica often spoke as though straight out of the end of his thoughts.

Manser's hand slowed over the ashet he was holding. "Yes we did, Adrian Laris, you used it a few moments ago."

"Did I? I don't know. But I'm positive Dorothy never told us. She almost refused to speak about him and you always said the solicitor never told you."

"The name's in his book-plate. It's sort of woven into the foliage. You must have seen it. I'll show you. Where's the book?"

"I'm not sure. I'll look later."

However, she did not look later. Either the thought went out of her head or, more probably, she did not wish to return to the morning-room where she had carefully replaced the copy of Petronius before locking the door.

As they were going to bed, Manser felt old. He was stiff, and restless, and chilly; but despite being well fed, sleep would not come. The curtains across the upright rectangle of the window were drawn back, and a cold April moon, low at the head of the valley, could be seen behind the branches of a still leafless tree. Was it rising or setting? The question had never been part of his world, and he asked in vain. But when he next turned over, the moon had gone, leaving only a hint of light behind clouds. In their old home there would have been the glimmer of street lamps, or sometimes the diminishing roar of a train on its way to London. Here a night bird of some sort was crying in the wood, and a wind moved restlessly about the house causing a loose casement in the room below to rattle in its frame. He turned over towards his wife. She seemed to be asleep. Outside a dog fox barked in the curiously unpleasant manner common to their kind. Again he moved restlessly and contemplated getting up to fix the window, but the night air was cold, and his bed was warm. With an effort he lay still, eventually drifting into a dream-infested sleep. He was looking at the stone inscription in the garden. As he looked, a round grey face emerged from below it, at first slowly; a head twisting this way and that like an obscene maggot, and becoming every instant more aggressive, a ball of activity like a storm of insects rushing at his face. He tried to step back to get away but fell among the brambles which pinioned his legs. The thing was cascading over him and flies poured into his mouth. With a grunt he was awake again, his hands somehow held in front of his face.

Manser was not an imaginative man and blamed himself for his bad dreams – too much port and Stilton at the end of the meal. His own fault! Monica was still asleep. Pale light glimmered at the window. The tapping in the room below had ceased. He buried his head impatiently in the pillow and as a consequence did not look out to see a thin grey figure, of whom the things of the night took no care as being one of themselves, detach itself from the oak wood and, like a shadow of something no bigger than a man's hand passing across the moon, move silently towards the garden and the unlighted house. When it reached the wall it was lost to sight in the dense foliage. A wren, disturbed from its roost, flew hastily to another part of the garden. Something white, with indistinct features that might have been a human face, hovered above the wall where the inscription was concealed. But of all this Manser saw nothing although he dreamed uneasily, and Monica was a little cold.

In the morning the wind was in the east, cutting up the valley into the front of the house with a bitter chill more like February than early spring, and the trees cast hard shadows in the intervals between sunless squalls of rain and sleet. There was no excuse to go shopping, no warm invitation to visit anybody or anything, nothing on the TV in its temporary abode in the kitchen, and no real possibility of going outside between showers to do anything useful. Not even letters or the daily paper could be expected until lunchtime, at the very end of the rural delivery. Monica pretended to read the March copies of various magazines but was unable to find interest or concentration. Manser pottered over his bank accounts and dreamed of other places. They took lunch almost in silence, each thinking the same thing about where they had brought themselves, but neither able to say anything because they thought that the other would think differently and be hurt.

"It's dried up a bit," said Manser. "What shall we do this afternoon?"

"I don't think I want to do anything. But I ought to have a go at the back room."

"Couldn't you just leave it?"

"No. I can't do that. I must at least clear it ready for the workmen. We can't let them in there as it is. It looks as though we haven't bothered to do anything with it."

"I'll help you later."

"No, you get something done outside. You need the air. You didn't sleep properly last night."

And so they parted, leaving things unsaid.

Manser had gone into the garden with one clear objective, an objective he had been mentally completing all morning. He intended to make way for the removal of the wall. There was something about it, he knew not what and didn't really care, which disturbed his sleep and upset his wife, and he didn't want Monica to see the face. It was too much like one he had observed her trying to conceal behind a cupboard in the cloakroom. A pity really. A lot of work would be needed to change everything, and in some respects the garden would have offered a better prospect from the house in its old form.

The actual removal of the rubbish that had grown up along the wall took a good deal longer than he anticipated; in recent years he had found things in gardens usually did. But the exercise kept him warm in the cold breeze coming up from the east, and it was lateish afternoon before he was working in front of the inscription itself. He was beginning to cut away the fish-bone fronds of cotoneaster when his eye was attracted by something near to the earth in front of where he knew the carved face to be located: not so much a thing as a vague dark patch. Although a seasoned gardener, Manser experienced a considerable reluctance to pull out whatever it was. Instead he grasped the long-handled lopping shears and attacked the cotoneaster at ground level. The steel bit easily through the gnarled stems, and the unsupported bush fell forwards towards him bearing cobwebbed pockets of discarded berries and the torn remains of abandoned nests.

Released from imprisonment between bush and wall, the object rolled slowly away from the stone revealing Dr Laris's face – well, somebody's face – in clear relief. But Manser's eyes were not on the face, although he later wished they had been. He stepped back carefully, perhaps informed by the prescience of dreams, and stared down at what appeared to be a ball of long dark hair, about the size of a large coconut, and like a coconut dense at the centre, loose and uncertain at the periphery. Before making any attempt to pick it up, Manser put on a pair of thick canvas gloves. Even then he hesitated. It *was* long hairs, and there was something whitish like a bundle of moths inside it. He poked with his foot. At that precise moment an eddy of wind must have blown up the valley giving the almost weightless mass an upward lift. To Manser, who was bending forward slightly, the thing appeared to run up his legs and into his face. With a cry of disgust he jumped back, flailing at the air to get it away. As he did so, laughter, unmistakably laughter, sounded from somewhere above and in front of him. But it was the sound he heard from the house which called him, and he neither looked up nor saw the thought-less wind toss the ball of hair over the wall and across the pasture, bounding and billowing, until it was lost to sight.

*

Monica had also formed plans for the afternoon. They involved mastering her aversion to the empty room and clearing out Dr Laris's abandoned rubbish, for so she had persuaded herself to think of his quite valuable collection of the Loeb Classical Library on the floor. Nevertheless, somehow she kept finding other little jobs to do about the house, and much of the afternoon had gone before she finally ran out of excuses.

With a lot of banging about she assembled brushes, dusters and a vacuum cleaner at the door, turned the key, drew a deep breath and, with a show of bravado she did not feel, went in. For a minute or two she was successfully indignant. It was absolutely ridiculous that such an effort was needed to undertake such a trivial domestic tidy-up. The atmosphere of the room enveloped her like night air. The spiders were back. Webs hung at the windows she had cleared only yesterday. But it was not spiders that bothered her. In her suburban existence she had thought of them as no more than a messy substitute for fly spray. It was not the spiders but the flies. Where could they all have come from? The corners of the ceiling were thick with them, while others fizzed and spun in their death throes on the window-sill and on the floor. She pulled in the vacuum cleaner with an ill-formed idea of sucking them up, and then found there was no electric point in the room; something they had not noticed previously. A dust pan and brush, quickly! She had no fly spray. Where were they coming from? Her eye lighted on the book she had put back after the party. It was crawling with flies. They were pouring out of it. This couldn't be! With a last frantic effort to rid herself of her rising fear and loathing she turned to the window intending to beat it and attract Peter's help. She saw him at once, at the far end, below the wall. For a measurable instant of time she stood incapable of sound or motion, suspended between incomprehension and horror. Then she screamed.

It was that terrible sound, so utterly uncharacteristic of his wife, that caused Manser to run back to the house as he had not run for years. He found her in the back porch, crouched against the wall, shaking like a child in fever, her eyes focused on something beyond him. He picked her up, surprised at his own strength, and she looked at him properly. "You're alright," she said, and held onto him very tightly, as she had not done for a long time.

When she told him, he could only grasp part of the story, but the four words she wept into his shoulder at the end were closer to him than the rest. "We must get away," she said. "I know," he replied without hesitation. "We made a mistake."

The departure of the Mansers from the district was immediate, complete and largely unexplained. Fortunately their son was eventually able to make an immensely profitable sale to the family of an eccentric conservationist whose sole concern was to restore the property as nearly as possible to the "original" condition in which Dr Laris had left it. It is perhaps unnecessary to remark that they lived at peace with the house and their neighbours (and live there to this day for ought I know).

The Mansers, having left at Monica's insistence on the very day of the horror, spent several nights recovering in the safe refuge of Ludlow, in one of the finest old hotels in England, before returning, somewhat bashfully, to live in a new home among their old familiars. They were, for the most part, very happy, although Monica did need some treatment at first for a nervous disorder which the psychiatrists found puzzling.

Miss Hunter smiled sweetly when she thought of them. Dr Laris had been such fun, even if he was sometimes a little mischievous, and he had so loved his garden. He had even translated his inscription for her so that Will Blackstone's account of it had felt quite familiar. The words were of course pagan, but not *wickedly* pagan. And she *had* promised to help him see that no harm came to his garden. The ball of black hair from the pony's tail had been so simple. It had been a lovely little touch to fold up one of the copies of the book-plate he had given her on the last day and put it inside the ball with the reference to Deuteronomy written on the back, "Cursed be he that removeth his neighbour's landmark." They could laugh over it together when the Mansers had gone. It made the whole thing quite Christian. And the Mansers weren't really country people at heart. They would be *so* much happier back in the life they knew and understood.

It took Monica a long time before she could bring herself to tell Peter exactly what she had seen when she looked for his help. His head, she said, was like a cloud of flies, and on the wall above him was what could have been a bare tree, but it had a face of sorts, and was dancing like death in a medieval morality play. But Peter only smiled condescendingly at her, and then abruptly ceased to find the picture amusing.

"I suppose," he began, but it was a little difficult for him to say exactly what he did suppose.